Erskine   Childers

German Influence on British Cavalry

Erskine Childers

German Influence on British Cavalry

ISBN/EAN: 9783337539801

Printed in Europe, USA, Canada, Australia, Japan

Cover: Foto ©Andreas Hilbeck / pixelio.de

More available books at **www.hansebooks.com**

GERMAN INFLUENCE ON BRITISH CAVALRY

BY

ERSKINE CHILDERS

AUTHOR OF
"WAR AND THE ARME BLANCHE," "THE RIDDLE OF THE SANDS,"
"IN THE RANKS OF THE C.I.V."
EDITOR OF VOL. V. OF "THE 'TIMES' HISTORY OF THE WAR"

LONDON
EDWARD ARNOLD

1911

Printed in Great Britain

PREFACE

<hr/>

THIS essay is meant to be read in connection with the facts

3

and arguments adduced in my book of last year, "War and the *Arme Blanche*," with its Introduction by Field-Marshal Lord Roberts. From the nature of the case I have not been able to avoid a small measure of repetition, but I have done my best to confine myself to new ground.

A word about my object in writing again. Contemporaneously with the publication of "War and the *Arme Blanche*," General von Bernhardi published in Germany his "Reiterdienst," and an English edition, translated by Major G.T.M. Bridges, D.S.O., under the title "Cavalry in War and Peace," appeared simultaneously in this country. Like its predecessor, "Unsere Kavallerie im nächsten Kriege" (translated under the title "Cavalry in Future Wars"), this new book by General von Bernhardi was headed with a highly laudatory Preface from the pen of General Sir John French, who commended it to military students in this country as a brilliant and authoritative treatise on the employment of Cavalry in modern war. It was included in the valuable "*Pall Mall* Series" of military books, published by Hugh Rees and Co.; and, in short, unless the critical faculties and native common-sense of Englishmen can be aroused, it is likely to become a standard work. There exists, be it remembered, no similar work, modern and authoritative, by a British author.

My object in this essay is to arouse those critical faculties and that common-sense. Without any disrespect to General von Bernhardi, who writes, not for Englishmen, but, as a German reformer, for what he regards as an exceptionally backward Cavalry, I wish to show, not only that we have nothing to learn even from him in the matter of Cavalry combat, but that, if we only have the pluck and independence to break off the demoralizing habit of imitating foreign models, and to build on our own war experience and our own racial aptitudes, we have the power

4

of creating a Cavalry incomparably superior in quality to any Continental Cavalry.

The indispensable condition precedent to that revival is to sweep away root and branch the tactical system founded on the lance and sword, and to create a new system founded on the rifle.

I shall endeavour to show, using von Bernhardi's "Reiterdienst," with Sir John French's Introduction, and our own official Manuals, as my text, that in the matter of modern Cavalry warfare no principles worthy of the name exist among professional men. The whole subject is in a state of chaos, to which, I believe, there is no parallel in all the arts of war and peace. And the cause of that chaos is the retention in theory of a form of combat which is in flagrant contradiction with the conditions exacted by modern firearms, and is utterly discredited by the facts of modern war.

The excellence of the translation furnished by Major Bridges has made it unnecessary for me to introduce into this essay the various terms and phrases used in the original German text. After a study of that text, I am satisfied, if Major Bridges will permit me to say so, that, obscure as the author's exposition often is, no part of the obscurity is due to the translator. I have not found a technical term of which he has not given the correct English equivalent, or a passage where he has not accurately interpreted the original sense.

Let me add that I have been encouraged further to write this essay by the keen and instructive controversy which followed the publication of my book of last year. Incidentally I have taken the opportunity in this volume to reply to some of the criticisms against its predecessor, and to clear up some points which I think were not fully understood.

E.C.

March, 1911.

CONTENTS

GERMAN INFLUENCE ON BRITISH CAVALRY

7

CHAPTER I

INTRODUCTORY

I. The German Model.

Impartial observers of the recent controversy upon the merits of the lance and sword as weapons for Cavalry must have been struck by one singular circumstance—namely, that there exists in our language no standard modern work upon the tactics and training of Cavalry in modern war, written by a Cavalryman, accepted by Cavalrymen, and embodying and illustrating the lessons of the two great modern wars waged since the invention of the long-range, smokeless magazine rifle. Without such a work, controversy is seriously hampered. The need for it is beyond dispute.

Whatever the extent of the revolution brought about by the magazine rifle, a revolution, by universal admission, there is. Since 1901 a serious firearm has been substituted for the old carbine formerly carried by the Cavalry, and the Cavalry Manual has been rewritten, with increased stress on the importance of fire. It is also the fact that, from whatever causes, the lance and sword have proved, both in South Africa and Manchuria, almost innocuous weapons. These facts demand, to say the least, serious recognition from those who still hold that the lance and sword are the most important weapons of Cavalry. Angry letters to the daily press, desultory and superficial articles in the weekly and monthly press, are not enough. What is wanted is some comprehensive and authoritative exposition of what Cavalry functions are in modern war, how they have been modified by the firearm, and why, with chapter and verse, not by way of vague allegation, the only great wars in which that firearm has been tested are to be regarded as "abnormal" and uninstructive.

8

For illumination and confirmation on these matters, we are constantly referred, in defence of the lance and sword, by our own Cavalry authorities to foreign countries whose armies have had no experience at all of modern civilized war as revolutionized by the modern magazine rifle. We are referred, above all, to Germany, and, in particular, to the works of a German officer, General von Bernhardi, who (1) writes exclusively for the German Cavalry, without the most distant reference to our own; (2) whose own war experience dates from 1870, when he fought as a Lieutenant, and who has not seen the modern rifle used in civilized war; (3) who believes that no wars, ancient *or modern*, except the American Civil War of 1861-1865, afford an analogy to modern conditions, and that the modern Cavalryman must base his practice on "speculative and theoretical reflection"; (4) who states that the German Cavalry, owing to indifference to the revolution wrought *by the modern firearm*, and excessive adherence to "old-fashioned knightly combats," is at this moment wholly unprepared for war and is trained on Regulations which, though quite recently revised, he makes the subject of stinging and sustained ridicule; (5) who is so ignorant of the technique of fire-action by mounted troops that he renders it, unconsciously, more ridiculous even than shock-action; and (6) who firmly believes in the lance and sword, and in the shock-charge as practised "in the times of Frederick the Great and Napoleon."

In this strange list of qualifications the reader will see the makings of a pretty paradox. And a pretty paradox it is, a bewildering, incomprehensible paradox; not so much, indeed, that a German author, born and bred in a German atmosphere, should be so saturated with obsolete German traditions that even in the act of denouncing them he can subscribe to them, but that British Cavalrymen, headed by Sir John French, our foremost Cavalry authority, men who have had three years' experience of war with the modern magazine rifle, who have *seen* the *arme blanche* fail and the rifle dominate tactics, and who, eight years before the German Cavalry even stirred in its sleep, acquiesced in changes in Cavalry armament and training directly based on that experience—that these men should acclaim the works of the aforesaid German author as the last word of wisdom on the tactics and training of modern Cavalry, and represent them as such to young British Cavalrymen, is a circumstance which almost passes belief.

Still, it is a fortunate circumstance. We have a body of doctrine to grapple with and controvert. If we succeed in dissipating the myth of German superior intelligence on Cavalry matters, we go a long way towards dissipating the whole of the *arme blanche* myth, which in the opinion of our greatest living soldier, Lord Roberts—an opinion founded on lifelong experience of war—is as mischievous a superstition as ever fettered a mounted military force. The whole of the material is here—and it is unexceptionable material for controversy—for Sir John French himself contributes his own views on the subject in the form of laudatory Introductions to both of General von Bernhardi's works.

I propose in the following pages (1) to criticize General Sir John French's views, so expressed; (2) to analyze and criticize General von Bernhardi's recently published work, "Cavalry in War and Peace," and to contrast his teaching with that of our own Service Manuals; (3) to try to show that each General refutes himself, that both refute one another, and that Sir John French is, by a strange irony, far more reactionary than the German officer to whom he directs us for "progressive" wisdom; (4) to expose the backwardness and confusion in every department of Cavalry thought, here and in Germany, as a direct consequence of the attempt to found a tactical system upon obsolete weapons; and (5) incidentally to put forward what I venture to suggest is true doctrine.

This doctrine, briefly, is that the modern Cavalry soldier is, for practical purposes, represented by three factors—man, horse, and rifle—and that it is only by regarding him strictly and constantly as a mounted, that is to say, an especially mobile, rifleman, as distinguished from the less mobile foot-rifleman, that we can establish his war functions on a simple, sound, and logical basis. I ask the reader to hold that clue firmly as a guide through the perplexities and obscurities of the topic and the obsolete terminology and phraseology which not only disturb reasoning but distort and enfeeble practice.

At the outset let the reader grasp the following historical facts as to the efficacy of swords and lances in civilized war:

1. Franco-German War of 1870-71: Six Germans killed and 218 wounded by the sabre and clubbed musket counted together. No separate figures for the lance. [Total German casualties from all weapons, 65,160.][1]

2. South African War, 1899-1902: No statistics as to *death*. About fifty Boer casualties through lance and sword together, and about fifty more prisoners taken. [Total Boer and British deaths, and wounds from all weapons, about 40,000.]

3. Russo-Japanese War, 1904-05: No exact figures, but apparently not more than fifty casualties from lance and sword together. [Total casualties in action, over 400,000.]

II. "CAVALRY IN FUTURE WARS."

Two works by General von Bernhardi have been translated into English, and widely circulated among our military men. I propose to say but little about the first, "Cavalry in

11

Future Wars," because I have already endeavoured to criticize it in detail in my own book, "War and the *Arme Blanche*." It is the second work, "Cavalry in War and Peace," published only in 1910, that I wish to make the basis of discussion in this volume; but in order to explain the history of German influence on British Cavalry, it is necessary to recall briefly certain features of its predecessor.

"Cavalry in Future Wars" was first published in German in 1899, before the Boer War broke out. There was a second edition in 1902, when the Boer War was drawing to a close, and this second edition, headed by General French's Introduction, was translated and published in England in 1906. It was a strange work, strangely sponsored. The keynote was fire-action for Cavalry, the moral drawn by the English sponsor shock-action for Cavalry. The chapters on fire-action, urging the adoption of a firearm even better than the Infantry rifle in substitution for a mere pop-gun, formed in themselves a complete refutation of shock; while the chapters on shock, so illogical and self-contradictory was the method of exposition, formed an equally complete refutation of fire-action.

It is true that the spirit of fire predominated, that fire was the General's message to his lethargic brother-officers, but the message was so strangely expounded that it is no wonder that for ten years they turned a deaf ear to it. Instead of telling them at the outset that if they themselves adopted a good firearm, and learnt to use it properly, they would immensely enhance the value of Cavalry for all the purposes of war, he opened his argument with a melancholy dirge over the departed glories of the Cavalry owing to the adoption by other classes of troops of the deadly modern firearm. They must recognize, he told them, that they had been "driven out of their place of honour on the battlefields of the plains"; that they could henceforward only attack

Infantry who were already so shattered and demoralized by the fire of other Infantry as to have reached the point of throwing away their arms, and much more in the same sense. Never was such a tactless prophet! And the pity of it was that he did not really mean all he said. What he meant was that the ancient glories of the *arme blanche*, when pitted against the firearm, were gone past recall—a circumstance scarcely worth an elegy, one would imagine, from a scientific soldier. War is business, not romance, and if the same or better results can be produced by an intelligent and dashing use of the firearm, it is waste of breath to lament the decay of the lance and sword. It was the main purpose of the General's work to prove that these results could be so obtained, and whenever he warmed to his subject, and fell into temporary oblivion of the romantic weapons, he proved his point well enough, in theory.

But, unfortunately, his oblivion of the lance and sword lasted only as long as he was criticizing the action of Cavalry against troops not armed with those weapons. When he came to the action of Cavalry against Cavalry, both by hypothesis armed, not only with the lance and sword, but also with the best modern rifle obtainable, the principle he had just established—namely, that the rifle imposes tactics on the steel—disappeared, and the opposite principle —that the steel imposes tactics upon the rifle—took its place. I say "principle," but in this latter case no reasoned principle based on the facts of war was expounded, because it seemed never to occur to the General that Cavalry in combat with Cavalry would have the bad taste to use their rifles.

Needless to say, it was impossible to sustain this daring paradox with any semblance of logic and consistency throughout a book dealing with all the phases of war. War is not a matter of definitions, but of bullets and shells. And, in fact, the General threw logic and consistency to the winds. In his fire-mood he unconsciously covered shock-tactics with ridicule, but in his shock-mood (no doubt, much to the relief of the victims of his wrathful invective in Germany) he conclusively demolished the principle of fire.

This was easily explicable. In the first place, the General was a German writing exclusively to Germans, to whom the bare idea of relying on the prosaic firearm seemed sacrilegious. Merely to implant that idea in their heads, to persuade them that the rest of the world was moving while they were asleep, was a vast enough aim for a German reformer—too vast an aim, indeed, as the event proved. In the second place, the General, so far as the effect of modern firearms was concerned, was working wholly in the realm of theory. When he first published his book those weapons had not been tested in civilized war. The most recent relevant war experience was that of 1870 and of the other European wars of that period, when the firearm was exceedingly imperfect. But even then, as he frankly and forcibly stated, it was in consequence of their neglect of this firearm, imperfect as it was, that the European Cavalry, the German Cavalry included, gave such a painfully poor account of themselves. He looked farther back, just as Colonel Henderson and many other critics in our own country looked back, to the brilliant achievements of American Cavalry in the Civil War of 1861-1865, mainly through the agency of the firearm. But here the firearm was still more primitive—a fact of which General von Bernhardi took no account. It was enough for him that inter-Cavalry shock survived through the Civil War, though the steel came to be wholly ineffective against Infantry. That forty years of scientific progress might have produced a weapon which would have banished shock in any form did not occur to him.

Nevertheless, there seemed to be good ground for the hope

14

that, when he came seriously to collate and examine the phenomena of the first great wars since the invention of the modern rifle—those in South Africa and Manchuria—he would find in the exact confirmation of his views on fire, and in the complete falsification of his views on shock, ground for a drastic revision of his whole work, with a view, not perhaps to a complete elimination of the steel weapons, but to their complete subordination to the rifle. It is true that the omens were not very favourable.

Between 1899 and 1902, when his second edition was published, a great mass of South African information became available, not in finished historical form, but in a form quite suitable for furnishing numberless instructive examples of the paramount influence of fire and the futility of the lance and sword. But the General made no use of these examples. He confined himself to a general allusion to the "very important data obtained in South Africa as to the employment of dismounted action by Cavalry" (p. 7), and in a later passage (p. 56) to some commendatory remarks on the "brilliant results" obtained through mounted charges made with the rifle only by the Boers in the latter part of the war. Unfortunately, it was plain that he had given no close technical study either to these charges or to the "important data" vaguely alluded to; otherwise he would have saved himself from many of the solecisms which abound in his work. Still, the fact remained that the war was unfinished when his second edition was published, while another great war broke out only two years later. It seemed not unlikely that mature reflection upon the incidents of these wars would ultimately tend to clarify and harmonize his views on shock and fire.

Meanwhile the English edition was published, with its Introduction by General Sir John French. By this time (1906) the events of our own war were fully collated and recorded, while the Manchurian War had also taken place. Instead of supplying a really useful commentary upon the German work, written from the point of view of British experience, instead of drawing attention to its deficiencies and errors, and pointing out how inevitable they were under the circumstances of its composition, General French hailed the work as a complete, final, and unanswerable statement of Cavalry doctrine. Von Bernhardi, he said, "had dealt with remarkable perspicuity and telling conviction and in an exhaustive manner with every subject demanding a Cavalry soldier's study and thought." How Sir John French's readers reconciled this effusive eulogy with the contents of the book remains a mystery. As I have said, the only really important feature of the book was the insistent advocacy of fire-tactics—and not merely defensive, but offensive fire-tactics—for Cavalry. This feature was minimized in the Introduction. In its place was a vehement attack on the advocates of fire-tactics in England, the truth of whose principles had just been signally demonstrated in our own war.

There was not a word about the "important data" to be derived from the war; not a word about the Boer charges, of whose terribly destructive effects Sir John French knew far more than General von Bernhardi. On the contrary, the war was dismissed in a few slighting and ambiguous sentences, as wholly irrelevant to the *arme blanche* controversy, in spite of the fact that, in direct consequence of the war, our Cavalry Manual had been rewritten and the Cavalry firearm immensely improved—facts which would naturally suggest that the war had been instructive.

Praise of Von Bernhardi, singular as the form it took, was by no means academic. In the next revision of our Cavalry Manual (1907) the compilers borrowed and quoted considerably from "Cavalry in Future Wars." And yet every sound principle in that work had years before been anticipated and expounded far more lucidly and thoroughly in the fascinating pages of our own military writer, Colonel Henderson, whose teaching had been ignored by the Cavalry of his own country.

FOOTNOTES:

[1] Report of German Medical Staff. No French figures available.

CHAPTER II

SIR JOHN FRENCH ON THE ARME BLANCHE

So the matter stood until, early in 1910, General von Bernhardi produced his second work, "Cavalry in War and Peace." An admirable English translation by Major G.T.M. Bridges promptly appeared, again with an Introduction by Sir John French.

It must, one might surmise, have given him some embarrassment to pen this second eulogy. The previous book had been "perspicuous," "logical," "intelligent," and, above all, "exhaustive and complete." Two wars, it is true, had intervened, but neither, according either to Sir John French or, we may say at once, to General von Bernhardi, was of any interest to Cavalry. What fresh matter, either for German exposition or for British eulogy, could there be? That is one of the questions I shall have to elucidate, and I may say here that the only new fact for General von Bernhardi is the recent promulgation of a revised set of Regulations for the German Cavalry, Regulations which, in his opinion, though "better than the old ones," are still almost as mischievous, antiquated, and "unsuitable for war" as they can possibly be, and whose effect is to leave the German Cavalry "unprepared for war." But this is not a new fact which could properly strengthen Sir John French in recommending the German author to the British Cavalry as a brilliantly logical advocate of the lance and sword, and it is not surprising, therefore, that the tone of his second introduction is slightly different from that of the first.

For the first time there appears a reference to the German Cavalry Regulations, from which the English reader would gain an inkling of the fact that General von Bernhardi is not a prophet in his own country, and that all is not harmony and enlightenment among the "progressive" Cavalry schools of Europe. On one specific point—raids—Sir John French "ventures to disagree" with General von Bernhardi, and he writes, also in quite general terms, that he does not "approve of all that the German Regulations say about the employment of Cavalry in battle." But even this latter note of criticism is very faint and deprecatory; nor is there anything to show that the writer, except on the one point mentioned, is not thoroughly at one with the German author's principles. The main purpose of this Introduction, as of the earlier one, is to claim that Bernhardi's book is a triumphant justification of the lance and sword. It is a "tonic for weak minds," an antidote against the "dangerous heresies" of the English advocates of the mounted rifleman, whose "appeals from ignorance to vanity" deserved scornful repudiation.

Once more, and in warmer language than ever, the General protests against the pernicious tendency to attach value to the lessons of South Africa; but this time, fortunately, he gives some specific reasons for regarding the war as "abnormal," and I shall devote the rest of this chapter to an examination of these reasons.

They are four: (1) That the "Boer commandos dispersed to

the four winds when pressed, and reunited again some days or weeks later hundreds of miles from the scene of their last encounter." This curious little summary of the war shows to what almost incredible lengths of self-delusion a belief in the *arme blanche* will carry otherwise well-balanced minds—minds, too, of active, able men like Sir John French, who have actually been immersed in the events under discussion. One fails at first to see the smallest causal relation between the phenomena of the war as he sets them forth and the combat value of the lance and sword, but the implied argument must be this: that these weapons could not be given a fair trial in combat because there was no combat, or, rather, only combat enough to cause the hundred casualties and prisoners for which, by the recorded facts, the lance and sword were accountable.

We figure a bloodless war, in which at the mere glimpse of a khaki uniform the enemy fled for "hundreds of miles"—at such lightning speed, moreover, that one of the chief traditional functions of the *arme blanche*, pursuit, was wholly in abeyance. Who would gather that there had been a "black week"; that Botha and Meyer held the Tugela heights for four months against forces between three and four times their superior in strength; that Ladysmith (where there were four Cavalry regiments) was besieged for four months, Kimberley for the same period, and Mafeking for seven months; that for at least nine months no "dispersion" took place even remotely resembling that vaguely sketched by Sir John French; and that during the whole course of the war no tactical dispersion took place which would conceivably affect the efficacy of the lance and sword as weapons of combat? A mere statement of the fact that the net rate of Boer retreat, even during the purely partisan warfare of 1901-02, was almost invariably that of ox-waggons (two miles an hour on the average), that until the last year of the war the Boers were generally accompanied by artillery, and that from the beginning of the war to the end not a single waggon or a single gun was ever captured through the agency, direct or indirect, of the lance and sword, shatters the hypothesis that these weapons had any appreciable combat value.

But that is only the negative side of the argument. We have to deal with a mass of plain, positive facts in favour of the rifle as an aggressive weapon for mounted troops. The Boer rifle caused us 29,000 casualties, over 40 guns and 10,000 men taken in action—losses which, to say the least, are evidence that some stiff fighting took place; for men who, when "pressed," run for "hundreds of miles" cannot take prisoners and guns.

We have before us the details of some hundreds of combats, in which Cavalry as well as other classes of troops were engaged, and the only effective way of testing the value of the steel weapons is to see what actually happened in these combats. The result of this inquiry is to show that the lance and sword were practically useless both in attack and defence, whatever the relative numbers and whatever the nature of the ground. No serious historian has ever attempted to make out any case to the contrary. No responsible man at the time would have ventured publicly to assert the contrary. It was patent to everybody—leaders and men—that the Boers were formidable because they were good mounted riflemen, and that our bitter need was for mounted riflemen as good as theirs. It is only when years of peace have drugged the memory and obliterated the significance of these events—melancholy and terrible events some of them—that it is possible to put forward the audacious claim that the lance and sword had no chance of proving their value because the Boers invariably ran away from them.

It must be evident that if this first reason for the failure of the lance and sword given by Sir John French is valid, it would be needless to proffer any others. And the others he does proffer only demonstrate further the weakness of his case. "Secondly," he says, "the war in South Africa was one for the conquest and annexation of immense districts, and no settlement was open to us except the complete submission of our gallant enemy." Such a campaign, he goes on to say, "is the most difficult that can be confided to an army," etc. Perfectly true—we agree; but what bearing has this obvious truth on the combat value of the lance and sword?

The issue before us is this: Is a certain mode of fighting possible in modern days? Is it practicable for men to remain in their saddles and wield steel weapons against men armed with modern rifles? "No," answers Sir John French, "it is not practicable, if your aim is annexation and the complete submission of a gallant enemy." Poor consolation for the unhappy taxpayer who pays for the maintenance of exceedingly expensive mounted troops, and commits himself to a scheme of conquest and annexation in the faith that these troops are efficient instruments of his will! Where would Sir John French's argument lead him, if he only followed it up and supplied the missing links? But that is the worst of this interminable controversy. Such nebulous arguments never are worked out in terms of actual combat on the battle-field.

Thirdly, says Sir John French, the horses were at fault. "We did not possess any means for remounting our Cavalry with trained horses...." "After the capture, in rear of the army, of the great convoy by De Wet, our horses were on short commons, and consequently lost condition, and never completely recovered it." This is an old argument, expressed in the old vague, misleading way. The war lasted nearly three years, beginning in October, 1899. The period referred to by Sir John French was in February, 1900. Long before this, when there was no complaint about the horses, the futility of the lance and sword, and the grave disabilities under which the Cavalry laboured owing to their inadequate carbine, had been abundantly manifest. The steel weapons may be said to have been obsolete after Elandslaagte, on the second day of the war.

At the particular period referred to by Sir John French — the period of the operations against Cronje and Kimberley — heat and drought did undoubtedly play havoc with all the horses in both armies, with those not only of the Cavalry, but of the mounted riflemen and Artillery on both sides. In February, 1900, a third of Cronje's small force was on foot, a pretty severe disability, since his whole force was scarcely equal to our Cavalry division alone, with its gunners and mounted riflemen included, while it was less than a quarter as strong as the whole army at the disposal of Lord Roberts. Sir John French makes use of a misleading expression when he says that "the Cavalry horses lost condition, and never completely recovered it." Nine-tenths of the horses here referred to succumbed altogether within a few months, and the Cavalry, like nearly all the mounted troops engaged in the operations in question, were completely remounted in June, for the grand advance from Bloemfontein to Pretoria.

During the succeeding two years of warfare all the mounted troops, Cavalry included, were several times remounted. So were the Boer troops, who, of course, had no remount organization at all for "trained" or untrained horses, and had to be content with anything they could pick up on the veldt. Yet, besides imposing fire-tactics on the Cavalry in every type of combat alike, they invaded the traditional sphere of Cavalry (and were imitated to some extent by our own Colonials and Mounted Infantry) by developing on

22

their own account a most formidable type of mounted charge, which during the last year of the war alone cost us 18 guns and 2,500 men killed, wounded, and prisoners. These charges were made with little rats of starveling ponies, whose extreme speed was scarcely that of the slow canter of an ordinary Cavalry charger.

If Sir J. French were to descend to statistics and facts, he would find it impossible to trace any causal relation between the efficacy of the lance and sword and the condition of the horses from time to time. The phenomena are precisely the same under all conditions from first to last. Everywhere and always the rifle is supreme. The better the horse, the better help for the rifle—that is all. In point of fact, he is quite aware that the principal success of the regular Cavalry was achieved when the horses were at their worst—that is to say, in the very period he refers to, when the Cavalry headed off Cronje and pinned him, purely by fire-action, to the river-bed at Paardeberg. Another good performance— though it was by no means specially a Cavalry performance; for mounted riflemen and Infantry were associated with the Cavalry—was the prolonged screening operations in front of Colesberg (November to January, 1900). There was no complaint about the horses then, but the sabre never killed or hurt a Boer. It was only once drawn from the scabbard, and was speedily resheathed, owing to hostile fire.

I pass to the last and strangest of Sir John French's reasons for regarding the war as abnormal in the sense that it gave no opportunity for the use of the lance or sword. It is this: That, "owing to repeated and wholesale release of prisoners who had been captured and subsequently appeared in the field against us, we were called upon to fight, not 86,000 or 87,000 men, but something like double that number or more, with the additional disadvantage that the enemy possessed on his second and third appearance against us considerable experience of our methods and a certain additional seasoned fitness." Here again is a proposition which alone is sufficient to destroy the case for the lance and sword. If, as a defence of those weapons, it means anything, it must mean that the Cavalry, by means of their steel weapons, were perpetually taking prisoners, to no purpose, because these prisoners were constantly released. Gradually the enemy learnt "experience of our methods," that is, of our shock-methods with the lance and sword, and, armed with this experience and the "seasoned fitness" produced by successive spells of fighting, they eventually countered or evaded those shock-methods, with what result we are not told. But such an interpretation is inadmissible. What Sir John French surely should say is precisely the reverse of what he does imply—namely, that we started the war in an ignorance of the Boer methods which cost us scores of millions of pounds; that we slowly learnt experience of those methods, and ultimately conquered the Boers and ended the war by imitating those methods. That is the plain moral of the war, as enforced by every historian.

Observe that, for the sake of argument, I am accepting as historically accurate Sir John French's statement about the advantage possessed by the Boers owing to the release of their prisoners. It is almost superfluous to add that the statement, in the sense he uses it, has no historical foundation. The truth is exactly the opposite. The advantage was immensely on our side. The Boers took many thousands of British prisoners, but permanently retained none, because they had no means of retaining them. During the last year of the war prisoners were released on the spot. A large proportion of these men fought again, some several times. No Boer prisoner of war—that is, captured in action —was released. In December, 1900, we had about 15,000 in our possession; in May, 1902, about 50,000.

24

It was mainly by this attrition of the Boer forces that we reduced them to submission. The element of historical truth in Sir John French's proposition is this: that in 1900, after the fall of Bloemfontein, a considerable number of Boers surrendered voluntarily, not in action, and were dismissed to their farms under a pledge not to fight again—a pledge which they broke, under circumstances into which we need not enter. There are no exact statistics as to the numbers of these men, but at an outside estimate they cannot have amounted to more than 5 per cent. of the total number of Boers engaged in the war. In any case, the point is totally irrelevant to the question of shock-tactics. That is a question of combat, and in combat, as Sir John French is aware, the Boers were, nine times out of ten, greatly outnumbered.

Such are Sir John French's reasons for the failure of the lance and sword in South Africa. They constitute an instructive revelation of the mental attitude of the advocates of those weapons. Is it not plain that we are dealing here with a matter of faith, not of reason; of dogma, not of argument; of sentiment, not of technical practice? The simple technical issue—what happens in combat?—is persistently evaded, and refuge sought in vague and inaccurate generalizations, which, when tested, turn out to throw no light upon the controversy.

Sir John French himself manages to demonstrate in this same Introduction that the question is really one of sentiment. It is a seemingly incurable delusion with him that the whole campaign on behalf of the rifle is an attack of a personal nature on the war exploits of himself and the regular Cavalry, instead of being, what it really is, an attack on the lances and swords carried by the Cavalry. This delusion carries him to the strangest lengths of professional egotism. In the whole of this Introduction there is not a line to indicate that any British mounted rifleman unprovided with steel weapons took part in the war, or that the tactics and conduct of these men have the smallest interest for Englishmen or the smallest bearing on the present controversy. No one would gather that our Colonial mounted riflemen led the way in tactical development, and frequently, brief and rough as their training had been, excelled the Cavalry in efficiency, simply because they were trained on the right principles with the right weapon.

"Even in South Africa," says Sir John French, "grave though the disadvantages were under which our Cavalry laboured from short commons and overwork" [as though these disadvantages were not shared equally by our mounted riflemen and by the Boers themselves!], "the Boer mounted riflemen acknowledged on many occasions the moral force of the cold steel, and gave way before it." Then follows a concrete instance, taken from the action of Zand River in May, 1900.

Anyone familiar with the history of the war must have felt deep bewilderment at the General's choice, for purposes of illustration, of this action, which has not generally been held to have reflected high credit on the Cavalry.

It is needless to discuss the battle in detail, because the accounts of it are set forth clearly and accurately enough in the "Official" and *Times* Histories, and, *inter alia*, in Mr. Goldman's work, "With French in South Africa." As a very small and unimportant episode in the battle, there was certainly a charge by a whole brigade of regular Cavalry against some Boers whom the *Times* History describes as a "party," and whom Mr. Goldman, who was present, estimates at 200 in number; but it is perfectly clear, from all accounts, (1) that the casualties resulting from the charge were too few to deserve record; (2) that the charge had no appreciable effect upon the fortunes of the day; (3) that the Cavalry on the flank in question suffered serious checks and

26

losses at the hands of a greatly inferior force; and (4) that Sir John French's turning force, like General Broadwood's turning force on the opposite flank, completely failed to perform the supremely important intercepting mission entrusted to them by Lord Roberts, and failed through weakness in mobile fire-action.

Sir John French's version of the action teems with inaccuracies. All the cardinal facts, undisputed facts to be found in any history, upon which the judgment of the reader as to the efficacy of the steel must depend, are omitted. There are no figures of relative numbers, no times, no description of the terrain, no statement of casualties. I will instance only one, but the greatest, error of fact. He writes that "the rôle of the Cavalry division was to bring pressure to bear on the right flank of the Boer army, in order to enable Lord Roberts to advance across the river and attack the main Boer forces."

This is a highly misleading account of Roberts's tactical scheme for the battle. Eight thousand Boers, disposed in a chain of scattered detachments, held no less than twenty-five miles of country along the north bank of the Zand River, their right resting on the railway, which ran at right angles to the river. We had 38,000 men, including 12,000 mounted men, of whom 5,000 were regular Cavalry. To have used the mounted Arm merely to "bring pressure to bear" upon the Boer flanks would have been a course altogether unworthy of Lord Roberts and the great army he controlled. He set no such limited aim before the Cavalry. He planned to surround and destroy the enemy by enveloping movements on both flanks, and gave explicit orders to that effect. French, with 4,000 men, had orders to ride round the Boer right flank, and seize the railway in their rear at Ventersburg Road. The same objective was given to the turning force under Broadwood, 3,000 strong, on the Boer

27

left. Both enveloping operations failed. To "press" the Boers into retreat was nothing. They must have retreated anyhow, in the face of an army five times their superior. The point was to *prevent* them from retreating into safety, to cut off their retreat, and with mounted turning forces together nearly equal to the whole Boer force this aim was perfectly feasible, given one condition, which was not fulfilled—that our mounted troops, headed by our premier and professional mounted troops, the Cavalry, could use their rifles and horses approximately as well as the Boers.

Now let us come to the heart of the matter.

Let us waive all criticism of the accuracy and completeness of Sir John French's narrative, and test the grounds of his belief that it was owing to their fear of the sword that the Boers gave way when Dickson's brigade charged. The Cavalry carried firearms as well as swords, and outnumbered the party charged by at least five to one. We cannot apply the test of casualties, because there were so few. The only test we can apply is that of analogy from other combats. Conditions similar to those of Zand River were repeated, on a smaller or larger scale, thousands of times. Do we find that steel-armed mounted troops had greater moral effect upon the enemy than troops armed only with the rifle? Did the presence of the lance and sword on the field of combat make any difference to the result? The answer, of course, is that it made no difference at all. Anyone can decide this question himself. We know precisely what troops were present, and how they were armed, in all the combats of the war.

We can detect many different factors at work, psychological, technical, tactical, topographical; but there is one factor which we can eliminate as wholly negligible, and that is the presence of the lance and sword. The same phenomena reappear whether those weapons are there or not. For

28

example, during Buller's campaign for the conquest of Northern Natal (May to June, 1900) very little use was made of regular Cavalry. During the first phase, the advance over the Biggarsberg, the six regiments of Cavalry at Buller's disposal were left behind at Ladysmith. The mounted work throughout was done mainly by irregulars. Was it of a less aggressive and vigorous character on that account, by analogy, say, with the mounted operations during the advance of Roberts from Bloemfontein to Pretoria? We find, on the contrary, that the results were better. The total relative numbers on the Boer side and our side were about the same: we were about four to one. But while Roberts had 12,000 mounted men, of whom 5,000 were Cavalry, Buller had only 5,500 mounted men, of whom 2,500 were Cavalry. Do we find that when the steelless irregulars mounted their horses, as Dickson's brigade mounted their horses, and made a rapid aggressive advance—"charged," that is—the Boers were any less inclined to retreat? On the contrary, they were more inclined to do so. Witness, for instance, Dundonald's long and vigorous pursuit with his irregular brigade over the Biggarsberg on May 14.

Or take the Bloemfontein-Pretoria advance, in which Zand River itself was an incident. Can we trace any further this alleged "terror of the cold steel"? Allowance must be made for the brief and inadequate training of the Mounted Infantry and Colonials; but, even with this allowance, a study of the facts shows that they did as well as the Cavalry, and sometimes better. The only effective local pursuit was made by Hutton's Australians at Klipfontein (May 30), where a gun was captured. These men had no steel weapons, yet they charged, and rode down their enemy.

Take Plumer's brilliant defence of Rhodesia with mounted riflemen. Take the relief of Mafeking, one of the most arduous and finely-executed undertakings of the war. Did the 900 troopers of the Imperial Light Horse who carried it out suffer from the lack of swords and lances? They would not have taken them at a gift. Did their work compare unfavourably with that of the Cavalry Division, 6,000 strong, in the relief of Kimberley? On the contrary, when we contrast the numbers employed, the opposition met with and the distance covered (251 miles in eighteen days), we shall conclude that the achievement of the irregulars was by far the more admirable of the two.

An infinity of illustrations might be cited to prove the same point, but, in truth, it is a point which stands in no need of detailed proof. The *onus probandi* lies on those who defend weapons which palpably failed. It is the Cavalryman's fixed idea that "mounted action," as the phrase goes, is associated solely with steel weapons; that soldiers in the saddle are only formidable because they carry those weapons. Mounted riflemen are pictured as dismounted, stationary, or as employing their horses only for purposes of flight. These fictions were blown to pieces by the South African War, and the irony of the case is that Sir John French gratuitously brings ridicule on the Cavalry by reviving them. If they are not fictions, the Cavalry stand condemned by their own pitifully trivial record of work done with the steel. But this is to slander the Cavalry. They do not stand condemned; their steel weapons stand condemned. They themselves, like all other mounted troops, did well precisely in proportion to their skill in and reliance on the rifle and horse combined. Their lances were soon returned to store; their swords, after rusting in the scabbards for another year, were also, in the case of nearly all regiments, abandoned; a good Infantry rifle replaced the weak carbine, and the Cavalry became definitely recognized as mounted riflemen.

No one has ever regarded Sir John French himself as otherwise than a leader of conspicuous energy and resource.

But, so far from owing anything to the lance and sword, he suffered heavily from the almost exclusive education of his troops to those weapons, and from the inadequacy of their firearm.

CHAPTER III

THE BRITISH THEORY OF THE ARME BLANCHE

AND now, what in Great Britain is the real theory on this question? Let us go to Sir John French again. The South African War, he says, is no guide for the future. It is abnormal, for the reasons stated above. The Manchurian War he has also stated to be abnormal. Where, then, is the theoretical advantage of the lance and sword over the modern rifle? We are left in ignorance. The physical problem is untouched. All we have is the bare dogmatic assertion that the steel weapon can impose tactics on the rifle. This is how Sir John French expresses the theory on p. xi of his Introduction: "Were we to do so" (*i.e.*, to "throw our cold steel away as useless lumber"), "we should invert the rôle of Cavalry, turn it into a *defensive* arm, and make it a prey to the first foreign Cavalry that it meets; for good Cavalry can always compel a dismounted force of mounted riflemen to mount and ride away, and when such riflemen are caught on their horses, they have power neither of offence nor defence, and are lost."

Eight years have elapsed since the Boer War. Memories are short, and it is possible now to print a statement of this sort, which, if promulgated during the dust and heat of the war itself, when the lance and sword fell into complete and well-merited oblivion, and when mounted men on both sides were judged rigidly by their proficiency in the use of the horse and the rifle, would have excited universal derision. The words which follow recall one of the writer's "abnormalities" already commented on: "If in European warfare such mounted riflemen were to separate and scatter, the enemy would be well pleased, for he could then reconnoitre and report every movement, and make his plans in all security. In South Africa the mounted riflemen were the hostile army itself, and when they had dispersed there was nothing left to reconnoitre; but when will these conditions recur?" When, indeed? There was nothing, it seems, to reconnoitre, because the enemy always "scattered and dispersed." And the Generals were "well pleased"! "Nothing left to reconnoitre"! One can only marvel at the courage of Sir John French in breathing the word "reconnoitre" in connection with Cavalry work in South Africa.

He ought to admit that Cavalry reconnaissance was bad, and that the army suffered for it. No historian has ever defended it. It was the despair of Generals who wanted information as to the position of the enemy. Wits apart, the rifle ruled reconnaissance, as it obviously always must rule it. *Ceteris paribus*, the best rifleman is the best scout. The Cavalry were not good riflemen, and were therefore not good scouts. Not a single Boer scout from the beginning to the end of the war was hurt by a sword or lance. Those weapons were a laughing-stock to foe and friend alike. And Sir John French's proposition is, not so much that the reconnaissance was good—presumably, that goes without saying—but that there was nothing to reconnoitre, thanks, apparently, to the terror spread by the lance and sword.

Such a travesty of the war may be left to speak for itself. But it is very important to comprehend the root idea which underlies it, an idea which, as we shall see, reappears in a less extreme form in General von Bernhardi's writings. It is expressed in the words "we should invert the rôle of Cavalry, turn it into a defensive arm." The rifle, it will be seen, is regarded as a *defensive* weapon, in contradistinction to the lance and sword, which are offensive weapons. To sustain this theory, it is absolutely necessary, of course, to proceed to the lengths to which Sir John French proceeds— to declare, in effect, that there was no war and no fighting; for if once we concede that there was a war, study its combats and compute their statistical results, we are forced to the conclusion that the rifle must have been used in offence as well as in defence. Abstract reflection might well anticipate this conclusion by suggesting that a defensive weapon and a defensive class of soldiers are contradictions in terms.

There must be two parties to every combat, and, unless there is perfect equilibrium in combat, one side or the other must definitely be playing an offensive rôle; and, even in equilibrium, both sides may be said to be as much in offence as in defence, whatever weapons they are using. The facts mainly illustrate the abstract principle. The Boers could not have taken guns and prisoners while acting on the defensive. Talana Hill, Nicholson's Nek, Spion Kop, Stormberg, Sannah's Post, Nooitgedacht, Zilikat's Nek, Bakenlaagte, were not defensive operations from the Boer point of view. Nor were Magersfontein, Colenso, Elandslaagte, Paardeberg defensive operations from the British point of view. Whether the rifles were in the hands of Infantry or mounted troops is immaterial. A rifle is a rifle, whoever holds it. It is just as absurd to say that the Boers who rode to and stormed on foot Helvetia and Dewetsdorp belonged to a defensive class of soldiers as it is to say that the Infantry who walked to and stormed Pieter's Hill belonged to a defensive class of soldiers. It is still more absurd to say that the Boers who charged home mounted at

Sannah's Post, Vlakfontein, Bakenlaagte, Roodewal, Blood River Poort, and many other actions, and the British mounted riflemen who did similar things at Bothaville, were performing a defensive function, while the Cavalry who pursued at Elandslaagte were performing an offensive function. Take this action of Elandslaagte, the solitary genuine example of a successful charge with the *arme blanche*. By whom was the real offensive work done? By the Infantry and by the Imperial Light Horse acting dismounted, and by the Artillery. After hours of hard and bloody fighting, these men stormed the ridge and forced the Boers to retreat. In the act of retreat they were charged by the Cavalry, who had hitherto been spectators of the action.

It might be objected that I am taking a verbal advantage of Sir John French. He is guilty, it may be argued, only of the lesser fallacy—that of thinking that the rifle is a defensive weapon for mounted men as distinguished from Infantry. Not so. He perceives the logical peril of admitting that the rifle is an offensive weapon for any troops, and in another passage, when deprecating attacks on the "Cavalry spirit" (p. vii), makes use of the following words: "Were we to seek to endow Cavalry with the *tenacity and stiffness* of Infantry, or take from the mounted arm the *mobility and the cult of the offensive* which are the breath of its life, we should ruin not only the Cavalry, but the Army besides." (The italics are mine.) It may be pointed out that, but for their firearms and the mobility and offensive power derived from them, the Cavalry in South Africa would indeed have been "ruined" beyond hope of rehabilitation.

But let us look at the underlying principle expressed. Infantry are "stiff and tenacious" (that is, obviously, in *defence*). Cavalry have the "cult of the offensive." Those are the distinctive "spirits" of the two Arms. The bitter irony of it! Which Arm really displayed the most "offensive spirit" in

34

South Africa? Study the lists of comparative casualties in the two Arms during that period of the war in which Infantry were mainly engaged. If at Talana, the Battle of Ladysmith, Colenso, Dronfield, Poplar Grove, Karee Siding, Sannah's Post, Zand River, Doornkop, or Diamond Hill, the Cavalry in their own sphere of work had shown the offensive power displayed by the Infantry in the battles on the Tugela, or in Methuen's campaign from Orange River to Magersfontein, or at Driefontein, Doornkop, Bergendal, and Diamond Hill, the war would have showed different results. There was no distinction in point of bravery between any branches of the Services. Fire-power and fire-efficiency were the tests, and lack of a good firearm and of fire-efficiency on only too many occasions fatally weakened the offensive spirit of the Cavalry.

And what of the "tenacity and stiffness" with which we must not "seek to endow" Cavalry? Ominous words, redolent of disaster! Have not they fully as much need of those qualities as Infantry? Imagine our Cavalry doing the work that the Boers had to do on so many score of occasions—to fight delaying rearguard actions against immensely superior numbers, with no reserves, and a heavy convoy to protect. We shall be fortunate if, through reliance on and skill in the use of the rifle, they display as much tenacity and stiffness as Botha's men at Pieter's Hill or Koch's men at Elandslaagte against forces four times their superior in strength, to say nothing of such incidents as Dronfield, where 150 Boers defied a whole division of Cavalry and several batteries; of Poplar Grove and Zand River, where small hostile groups virtually paralyzed whole brigades; or of Bergendal, where seventy-four men held up a whole army. There was nothing abnormal tactically or topographically about any of these incidents. Any function performed by the Boer mounted riflemen may be demanded from our Cavalry in any future war. Suppose them, for example, vested with the strictly normal duty of covering a retreat against a superior force of all arms; suppose a squadron, like the seventy-four Zarps at Bergendal, ordered to hold the cardinal hill of an extended position, and their leader replying: "This is not our business. We are an offensive Arm. We cannot entrench, and we have not the tenacity and stiffness of Infantry. Our business is to charge with the lance and sword." Would the General be well pleased?

The reader will ask for the key to this curious discrimination between the "spirits" of Cavalry and Infantry. It is this: The lance and sword, *when pitted against the rifle*, can, if they are used at all, only be used in offence. Men sitting on horseback, using steel weapons with a range of a couple of yards, plainly cannot defend themselves against riflemen. Even the Cavalry tacitly admit this principle, and if they accepted its logical consequence, a logical consequence completely confirmed by the facts of modern war, they would admit, too, that the sword and lance cannot be used for offence against riflemen in modern war. But they will not admit that. "Tant pis pour les faits," they say. "All modern war is abnormal. Our steel weapons dominate combat. Without them we are nothing."

In these circumstances they are forced to set up this strange theory—that Cavalry is a peculiarly "offensive" Arm, a theory which the reader will find expressed in all Cavalry writings. On the face of it the theory is meaningless. It is a mere verbal juggle, because, as I said before, there are two parties to every combat, and defence is the necessary and invariable counterpart of offence. All combatant soldiers, including Cavalry, carry firearms, and if Cavalry choose to use these firearms in offence, by hypothesis they will impose fire-action on the defence, whether the defence consists of

36

Cavalry or any other class of troops. Conversely, if they use their rifles in defence, as by hypothesis they must, they will impose fire-action on the attacking force, be it Cavalry or any other Arm. In other words, the rifle governs combat. That is why the lance and sword disappeared in South Africa. Both in offence and defence the Boer riflemen forced the Cavalry to accept combat on terms of fire.

And what kind of Cavalry do our Cavalrymen count upon meeting in our next war? They count, incredible as it seems, upon meeting Cavalry not superior, but inferior, to the Boer mounted riflemen, inferior because, as I shall show from von Bernhardi, they defy science, shut their eyes to the great principle of the supremacy of fire, are prepared deliberately to abdicate their fire-power, and hope to engage, by mutual agreement, as it were, and on the understanding that suitable areas of level ground can be found, in contests of crude bodily weight.

And what of the action of Cavalry against other Arms? We know Sir John French's opinion about mounted riflemen. They will gallop for their lives "defenceless" at the approach of "good" Cavalry. But Infantry, riflemen without horses, who cannot gallop, but can only run? Their case, it would seem, must be still more desperate. They are not only defenceless, but destitute even of the means of flight. And yet even Sir John French credits them, if not with an offensive spirit, at least with "tenacity and stiffness," derived, of course, from their rifles. But their mounted comrades, armed with these same rifles, lack these soldierly qualities. We arrive thus at the conclusion that the horse, which one would naturally suppose to be a source of immensely enhanced mobility and power, is a positive source of danger to a rifleman unless he also carries a lance or sword.

Here is the *reductio ad absurdum* of the *arme blanche* theory, and I beg for the reader's particular attention to it. Of course, the conclusion is in reality too absurd; for Sir John French himself does not really believe that Infantry are a defensive Arm. In point of fact, no serious man believes that Infantry in modern war have anything whatever to fear from the lance and sword, and their training-book is written on that assumption. Nor does Sir John French really believe that Mounted Infantry are a defensive Arm who run from Cavalry; otherwise, he would never rest until he had secured the complete abolition of our Mounted Infantry, who are now, under his official sanction, designed to act, not only as divisional mounted troops against steel-armed Continental Cavalry, but to co-operate with, and in certain events take the place of, our own regular Cavalry in far wider functions, and are presumably not going to be whipped off the field at the distant glimpse of a lance or sword. And I may say here that the reader can obtain no better and more searching sidelight on the steel theory than by studying the Mounted Infantry Manual (1909) for the rules given about similar and analogous functions. Nor, if Sir John French went the whole length of the theory, would he, as Inspector-General, have permitted our Colonial mounted riflemen to think that they might be of some Imperial value in a future war. It is only in order to sustain his *a priori* case for the steel weapons that he finds himself forced into the logical *impasses* to which I have drawn attention.

There is one further point to deal with before leaving Sir John French's Introduction. He admits the necessity of a rifle for Cavalry, and we may presume him to admit that the Boer War proved the necessity for a good rifle and the futility of a bad carbine. When, in his opinion, is this rifle to be used? "I have endeavoured to impress upon all ranks," he writes on page xvii, "that *when the enemy's Cavalry is overthrown*, our Cavalry will find more opportunities of using the rifle than the cold steel, and that dismounted attacks will be more frequent than charges with the *arme blanche*. By no means do I rule out as impossible, or even unlikely, attacks by great bodies of mounted men against other arms on the battle-field; but I believe that such opportunities will occur comparatively rarely, and that undue prominence should not be given to them in our peace training." (The italics are mine.)

This is a typically nebulous statement of the combat functions of Cavalry in modern war, and, like the generality of such statements, will be found to contain, if analyzed, a refutation of the writer's own views on the importance of the *arme blanche*. We ask ourselves immediately why he thought it necessary to account for the failure of the *arme blanche* in South Africa by the elaborate accumulation of arguments for "abnormality" developed a few pages earlier. After all, it seems, the war, in its bearing upon the efficacy of weapons, was normal. The Boers had no "Cavalry" in the writer's use of the word—that is, steel-armed Cavalry. What he assumes to be the primary and most formidable objective of our own steel-armed cavalry was, therefore, by a fortunate accident, non-existent. There was no need to "overthrow" it, because there was nothing to overthrow, and our Cavalry was free from the outset to devote its attention to the "other Arms"—that is, to riflemen and Artillery—assumed evidently by the writer to be a secondary and less formidable objective. But here, apparently, "opportunities" for the *arme blanche* are to occur "comparatively rarely" in any war, European or otherwise, whether the riflemen show "tenacity and stiffness" or "disperse for hundreds of miles"; whether the horses are perennially fresh or perennially fatigued; whether we outnumber the foe or they outnumber us; whether annexation or mere victory is our aim.

If only, we cannot help exclaiming, this principle had been recognized in 1899! We knew the Boers had no swords or lances: we had always known it. If only we had prepared our Cavalry for the long-foreseen occasion, trained them to fire, given them good firearms, and impressed upon them that opportunities for shock would occur "comparatively rarely," instead of teaching them up to the last minute that fire-action was an abnormal, defensive function of their Arm, worthy of little more space in their Manual than that devoted to "Funerals," and much less than that devoted to "Ceremonial Escorts."

The root of the fallacy propounded by Sir John French lies in his refusal to recognize that a rifle may be just as deadly a weapon in the hands of Cavalry as in the hands of "other Arms," and, indeed, a far more deadly weapon, thanks to the mobility conferred by the horse. If, for example, Infantry can, as he tacitly admits they can, force Cavalry to adopt

40

fire-action, *a fortiori* can Cavalry, if they choose, force Cavalry to adopt fire-action. In other words, the rifle governs combat, as it did, in fact, govern combat in South Africa and Manchuria. But Cavalry operating against Cavalry, according to Sir John French, are not so to choose. We can only speculate upon what may happen if one side is so unsportsmanlike as to break the rules and masquerade as another Arm. The stratagem is simple, because the rifle kills at a mile, and the orthodox Cavalry may be unaware until it is too late that the unorthodox Cavalry is playing them a trick. Meanwhile the best riflemen, whether they have horses or not, *will win*, and horsemen who have spent 80 or 90 per cent. of their time in steel-training will have cause to regret their error.

But Sir John French contemplates no such awkward contingencies. We may surmise, however, that it is owing to an uncomfortable suspicion of his own fallacy that in this paragraph and elsewhere he is so careful to isolate inter-cavalry combats from mixed combats, and to postulate the complete "overthrow" of one Cavalry—an overthrow effected solely by the *arme blanche*—before permitting the surviving Cavalry, in Kipling's words, to "scuffle mid unseemly smoke." He has a formula for the occasion. In this paragraph it is "when the enemy's Cavalry is overthrown." On page xiv, speaking of raids, which he deprecates, he says: "Every plan should be subordinate to what I consider a primary necessity—the absolute and complete overthrow of the hostile Cavalry"; and on page xv: "If the enemy's Cavalry has been overthrown, the rôle of reconnaissance will have been rendered easier," a truism upon which the Boer War throws a painfully ironical sidelight.

If the reader is puzzled by this curiously superfluous insistence on the "overthrow" of the enemy analogous to the equally superfluous insistence on the "offensive" character of the Cavalry Arm, he will once more find an explanation in the anomalous status of the *arme blanche*. No one would dream of repeatedly impressing upon Infantry, for example, as though it were a principle they might otherwise overlook, that their primary aim must be the absolute and complete overthrow of the hostile Infantry. But the advocate of the *arme blanche* is always on the horns of a dilemma. He dare not admit that the rifle in the hands of Cavalry is as formidable a weapon as in the hands of Infantry, if not a far more formidable weapon. He therefore instinctively tends to picture steel-armed Cavalry as perpetually pitted against steel-armed Cavalry. Both sides are always in offence until the moment when one is "completely and absolutely overthrown." Then some other rôles, very vaguely delineated, open up to the victor. Needless to say, this picture bears no resemblance to war. Troops are not, by mutual agreement, sorted out into classes, like competitors in athletic sports. Every Arm must be prepared to meet at any moment any other Arm, *and any other weapon.*

Nor do these "complete and absolute" obliterations of one Arm by its corresponding Arm ever, in fact, happen. That they could ever happen through the agency of the lance and sword is the wildest supposition of all. Compared with rifles, these weapons are harmless. Even the most backward and ignorant Cavalry, trained to rely absolutely on the lance and sword, would, if it found itself beaten in trials of shock, or, like the Japanese Cavalry, greatly outnumbered, resort to the despised firearm, imitate the tactics and vest itself with something of the "tenacity and stiffness," as well as with the aggressive potency, of those "other Arms," which, by hypothesis, must be attacked with the rifle; and in doing so it would force its antagonist to do the same.

CHAPTER IV

CAVALRY IN COMBAT

I. Instruction from History.

I HAVE gone at considerable length into the opinions of Sir John French, as expressed in his Introduction to von Bernhardi's work—partly because it is more important for us to know what our own Cavalrymen think than what German Cavalrymen think, and partly because it will be easier for the reader to estimate the value of the German writer's views if he is already familiar with Sir John French's way of thinking. We should expect, of course, to find identity between the views of the two men, since Sir John French acclaims the German author as the fountain of all wisdom; but on that point the reader would be well advised to reserve judgment.

I shall now discuss "Cavalry in War and Peace," and first let me say a few more words on a very important point—the circumstances of its composition.

When General von Bernhardi wrote his first book, "Cavalry in Future Wars," he did not take the current German Cavalry Regulations as his text, because they were too archaic to deserve such treatment. He condemned them in the mass, and, independently of them, penned his own scheme for a renovated modern Cavalry. After about nine years of complete neglect, during which the two great wars in South Africa and Manchuria were fought, the German authorities decided that some recognition of modern conditions must be made. They have recently re-armed the Cavalry with a good carbine, and issued a new book of Cavalry Regulations. These circumstances induced the General to write his second book, "Cavalry in War and Peace," and to throw it into the form of a direct criticism of the official Regulations, which he constantly quotes in footnotes and uses in the text of his own observations and constructive recommendations.

What is the result? The first point to notice is that he regards the new official Regulations, "though better than the old ones," as thoroughly and radically bad. His writings, he says, "have fallen on barren soil." He condemns them almost invariably for precisely the same reason as before, namely, that they virtually ignore the rifle in practice, and continue the ancient and worn-out traditions of the steel, with mere lip-service to the modern scientific weapon. But a disappointment was in store for those who had hoped that the mental process involved in criticizing concrete Regulations, as well as the vast mass of instructive phenomena presented by the two wars which, when he wrote first, were still "future wars" to him, would arouse the General himself to a realization of the inconsistencies in his own earlier work.

These hopes have been falsified. The fascination of the *arme blanche* was proof against the test, and the result is one of the strangest military works which was ever published. Bitter satire as it is on the official system of training, any impartial reader must end by sympathizing, not with the satirist, but with the officials satirized. They at any rate try to be logical. Their concessions to fire are the thinnest pretence; their belief in shock undisguised and sincere. Whatever follies and errors this belief involves them in, they pursue their course with unflinching consistency, sublimely careless of science and modern war conditions.

Their critic, on the other hand, keenly alive to the absurdities inculcated, has not the mental courage to insist on the only logical alternatives. Faced with the necessity of proving their absurdity, he refuses to use the only effective weapon available, gives away his own case for fire by weak concession to shock, and succeeds in producing a work which will convince no one in Germany, and the greater part of which, as a practical guide to Cavalrymen, in this country or any other, is worthless. A mist of ambiguity shrouds what should be the simplest propositions. We move through a fog of ill-defined terms and vague qualifications. We puzzle our brains with academical distinctions, and if we come upon what seems to be some definite recommendation, we are pretty sure to find it stultified in another chapter, or even in the same chapter, by a reservation in the opposite sense. The key to each particular muddle, to each ambiguity, to each timid qualification, to each confusing doctrinaire classification, is always the same—namely, that the writer, from sheer lack of knowledge of what modern fire-tactics are, at the last moment shrinks from his own theories about their value. What has happened is exactly what one would expect to happen. In Germany the General admits his failure, and in England he is hailed by Sir John French, who politely ignores his blunders about fire-action, as the apostle of the steel, instead of what he really is, the apostle, though the ineffectual apostle, of the rifle.

Let us first be quite clear as to his opinion of the present German Cavalry. "While all other Arms have adapted themselves to modern conditions, Cavalry has stood still," he says on the first page of his Introduction. They have "no sort of tradition" for a future war (p. 5). Their training creates "no sound foundation for preparation for war." It is "left far behind in the march of military progress." "It cannot stand the test of serious war." It is trammelled by the "fetters of the past," and lives on "antiquated assumptions" (p. 6). Its "mischievous delusions" will result in "bitter disappointment" (p. 175). Many of the new Regulations "betoken failure to adapt existing principles to modern ideas" (p. 361); others "do not take the conditions of reality into account"; or "cannot be regarded as practical"; or are "provisional"; and of one set of peculiarly ludicrous evolutions he uses the delightful phrase that they are "included in the Regulations with a view to their theoretical and not for their practical advantages" (p. 333). He stigmatizes "the formal encounters," the "old-fashioned knightly combats," the *pro forma* evolutions," the "survivals of the Dark Ages," the "spectacular battle-pieces," the "red-tape methods," the "tactical orgies," the "childish exercises," and "set pieces" of peace manœuvres. The origin of the trouble, he says, is "indolent conservatism" (p. 366). "Development in our branch of the Service has come to a standstill" (*ibid.*). The officers do not study history or the progress of foreign Cavalries. And he reiterates again and again his general conclusion that the Cavalry is unprepared for war.

Such is the material which forms his text. And we may ask at once, is a book based on such an appalling state of affairs, and addressed exclusively to a Cavalry described as being given over to ancient shibboleths, mischievous delusions and antiquated assumptions—is such a book likely to deserve the effusive and unqualified praise of our own foremost Cavalry authority? Is it likely to be worthy of becoming the Bible of a modern and progressive Cavalry, such as Sir John French considers our own Cavalry, trained under his own guidance, to be? Is it likely to be "exhaustive," "convincing," "complete"?

To suppose so is to insult the intelligence of our countrymen. We do not teach the ABC in our Universities. Our natural science schools do not assume that their pupils belong to the "Dark Ages," and waste two-thirds of their energy in laborious refutations of such extinct superstitions as witchcraft. The education of our sailors to modern naval war is not conducted on the assumption that the Navy consists of wooden sailing-vessels whose inadequacy to modern conditions must be elaborately demonstrated. A gunnery course—and the reader will note the analogy—does not consist mainly of arguments designed to prove that the cutlass is no longer so important a weapon as the long-range gun and the torpedo. Nor—in the military sphere—are our Infantry and Artillery instructed with a view to weaning them from the cult of the pike and the catapult.

So, too, we may be quite sure that there is something radically wrong when our Cavalry, in their search for an authoritative exposition of modern Cavalry tactics, are reduced to relying on a foreign writer who writes for a Cavalry ignorant of the elements of modern Cavalry tactics, and a good half of whose work is taken up with scoldings and appeals which from our British point of view are grotesquely redundant. All that is good in what von Bernhardi says about fire-action we know from our own war experience. All his errors about fire-action we can detect also from our own war experience.

We should expect Sir John French to comment on these facts, to warn his readers that the book under review was written for a Cavalry unversed in modern war and blind to its teaching. We should expect some note of pride and satisfaction in the fact that his own national Cavalry did not need these scathing and humiliating reminders that war is not a "theoretical" and "childish" pastime, but a serious and dangerous business; some hint to the effect that perhaps we, with our three years' experience of the modern rifle, may have something useful to tell General von Bernhardi about principles which he has framed in the speculative seclusion of his study. Not a word, not a hint of any such warning or criticism. The topic is too dangerous. Once admit that South Africa counts—to say nothing of Manchuria—once begin to dot the "i's" and cross the "t's" of the German's speculations,

47

and the *arme blanche* is lost. Instead, we have the passionless reservation from Sir John French that "he does not always approve" of those German Regulations, so many of which von Bernhardi thinks prehistoric and ludicrous, and at the end of his Introduction we have a fervent appeal to the British Cavalry not to "expose our ignorance and conceit" by overvaluing our own experience, but to "keep abreast with every change in the tendencies of Cavalry abroad," and to "assimilate the best of foreign customs" to our own. "Keep abreast!" What an expression to use in such a connection! "Best foreign customs!" Where are these customs? There appears to be only one answer—namely, that these customs are in reality the very customs which von Bernhardi attacks with such savage scorn, and yet by such ineffective and half-hearted methods that he leaves them as strong as before. His qualifications and reservations give Sir John French a loophole, so that what, read through English eyes, should be a final condemnation of the steel becomes to him a vindication of the steel.

The link between the two writers is that both disregard the facts of modern war. Since these facts are fatal to the steel theory, both are compelled to disregard them. What wars, then, according to the German expert, are the uneducated German Cavalry to study? He deals with this point on page 5. He dismisses the wars of Frederick the Great and Napoleon. He dismisses the Franco-German War of 1870-71, as we might expect from his earlier work, where he pointed out how meagre and feeble were the performances of the Cavalry compared with those of other Arms. He dismisses the Russo-Turkish War for the same reason, and, by implication, the Austro-Prussian War of 1866. All these wars, he says, "present a total absence of analogy." Then, entirely disregarding the whole period in which science perfected the firearm, he dismisses the wars in South Africa and Manchuria. And he comes back to what? The American War of Secession of 1861-1865, which "appears to be the most interesting and instructive campaign for the service of modern Cavalry," but which is "almost unknown" in Germany. In any other branch of study but that of Cavalry an analogous recommendation would be received with a compassionate smile. The element of truth and sense in it—and there is much truth and sense in it—is so obvious and unquestioned as not to need expression for the benefit of any well-informed student. The American horsemen discovered that the rifle must be the principal weapon of Cavalry, and through that discovery made themselves incomparably more formidable and efficient in every phase and function of war than the European Cavalries, who ignored and despised the American example in the succeeding European struggles. So far the writer is on the sound ground of platitude.

But has nothing notable happened since 1865? A very important thing has happened. The Civil War firearm is now a museum curiosity. Science has devised a weapon of at least five times the power—smokeless, quick-firing, and accurate up to ranges which were never dreamt of in 1865. Even the American weapon reduced shock to a wholly secondary place, and gave fire unquestioned supremacy. The modern weapon has eliminated shock altogether, and inspired new and far more formidable tactics—just as mobile, just as dashing, just as fruitful of "charges," but based on fire. Von Bernhardi cannot bring himself to contemplate this result. He must have his lances and swords, and is compelled therefore to go back to 1865, when the death-knell of those weapons was already being sounded; and in doing so he writes his own condemnation.

This is how his book opens: "The great changes which have taken place in military science *since the year 1866* have forced all arms to adopt new methods of fighting. It was first and foremost *the improvement in the firearm* which wrought the transformation on the battle-field." (My italics.) Since the year 1866! And yet the Cavalry are to go back to a war prior to that year for their instruction, and are to neglect the only wars in which the improved firearm has been tested! In point of fact, General von Bernhardi shows no sign of having closely studied even the American War of 1861-1865 with a view to finding out how the Americans used their firearms in conjunction with their horses. On this vital technical matter he writes throughout from a purely speculative standpoint, without a single allusion to the American technical methods, much less to the methods of our own and the Boer mounted riflemen of 1899-1902.

We must add in fairness that the General seems to be conscious that a war half a century old cannot be implicitly relied on for instruction, and he concludes his historical remarks, therefore, by the depressing conclusion that "there remains, then, nothing for us—with no practical war experience to go on—but to create the groundwork of our methods of training from theoretical and speculative reflection."

On this question of the most instructive war for Cavalry study Sir John French preserves an eloquent silence. He dismisses South Africa and Manchuria, but he does not echo the recommendation as to America. Thereby hangs a tale. For years before the South African War, for years before von Bernhardi was heard of in England, the ablest military historian of our time, the late Colonel Henderson, had been dinning the moral of America into the ears of our Cavalry authorities, without producing the smallest effect. His prophecies were abundantly justified—more than justified, for he wrote on the basis of the rifle of 1865, and the rifle of 1899 totally eliminated the shock-tactics which were still practicable in 1865. He died in 1902, before the Boer War was over, but in one of the last essays written before his death he told the Cavalry that shock was extinct. "Critics of the Cavalry work in South Africa," he says, "do not seem to have realized that the small bore and smokeless powder have destroyed the last vestiges of the traditional rôle of Cavalry" ("Science of War," p. 376).

It can be readily understood, therefore, that to refer our Cavalry of the present day to Colonel Henderson's brilliant and learned writings upon the American Civil War, would be a course highly dangerous to the interests of the lance and sword. Sir John French confines himself to urging his subalterns to read such "acknowledged authorities" as Sir Evelyn Wood and General von Bernhardi. But why is Sir Evelyn Wood singled out? Eminent as he is, he has not the requisite modern war experience. Why not Lord Roberts, who has, and who is the only living British officer with a European reputation? General von Bernhardi himself has not been on active service since 1870, when he served as a Lieutenant in the war against France. Sir John French will not advance the cause of the *arme blanche* in that way. He cannot stifle knowledge by an index. He need not agree with Lord Roberts, but to ignore him when speaking of "acknowledged authorities," to accuse him by implication of making "appeals from ignorance to vanity," is unworthy of Sir John French. If he believes in his cause, let him urge the Cavalry to hear both sides; it can do no harm. For my part, I would most strongly urge every Cavalry soldier to read von Bernhardi and Sir John French.

II. — General Principles of Combat.

To return to the book under discussion. Is it possible to gain from it any clear and definite idea of the respective functions and the relative importance of the rifle and the lance and sword as weapons for Cavalry? Unfortunately, no.

We have to deal with hazy generalizations scattered over the whole volume, each with its qualification somewhere else. It is true that warnings against the use of the steel greatly preponderate; and although, by selecting quotations from various chapters, each party to our controversy could easily claim the General as an adherent to his cause, the advocates of the rifle could certainly amass more favourable texts. The following passage might almost be regarded as conclusive —"We must be resolute in freeing ourselves from those old-fashioned knightly combats, which have in reality become obsolete owing to the necessities of modern war" (p. 111)—if its teaching were not weakened by such a maxim as this: "The crowning-point of all drill and of the whole tactical training is the charge itself, as on it depends the final result of the battle" (p. 325). But let us get closer to his actual argument. The reader should carefully study pp. 101 to 105, where, under the heading "B.—The Action of Cavalry" and sub-heading "1.—General," the author discusses in close detail the action of "Cavalry in the fight." The reader may wonder why he should have to wait till the hundredth page for this discussion. With the exception of some introductory pages, whose general sense, on the question of weapons, is against the lance and sword, the greater part of the first hundred pages are devoted to "Reconnaissance, Screening, and Raids," functions none of which, least of all the third, can be performed without fighting, or at least the risk of fighting, while fighting cannot be performed without weapons. The reason probably is that the author, in arranging his scheme, instinctively tended, like all Cavalry writers, to regard reconnaissance as a sphere where Cavalry can confidently rely on meeting only Cavalry of exactly the same stamp as themselves, and where combats will as a matter of course be decided in the old knightly fashion by charges with steel.

Such a state of things has no resemblance to real war. Raids, for example, are invariably levelled against fixed points and stationary detachments. The author himself is acutely aware of this truth, as we shall see hereafter; but the postponement of the topic of weapons until the middle of the book is typical of the confused arrangement of the whole, a confusion attributable to the ubiquity of the rifle in all combats and the insuperable difficulty of supposing it to be an inferior weapon to the steel.

It is impossible, therefore, to adhere strictly to the order in which the author arranges his treatise. I shall begin with the general chapter just referred to, and proceed, as far as possible, according to his own order from that point onwards.

First of all, he finds it necessary to reject the plan of "dividing tactical principles according to the idea of the pre-arranged battle and the battle of encounter," a course which gives one an insight into the lifeless pedantry he has had to combat in the branch of military science he has made his own. Unfortunately, his own classification, so far as it bears upon weapons, is little better. He distinguishes the "great battle," in which "the fighting is always of a pre-arranged nature," from "the fight of the independent Cavalry," where "it is possible to distinguish between an encounter and an arranged affair." This is vague enough, but what follows is vaguer. One infers that there is to be little or no shock in the "great battle," where the Cavalry "must conform to the law of other arms in great matters and small." And then he goes on: "But the fight is deeply influenced even in the former case [i.e., in the combats of the independent Cavalry] by the co-operation of these other arms, and I believe that only in exceptional cases will a purely Cavalry combat take place—at all events, on a large scale. When squadrons, regiments, and perhaps even brigades, *unassisted by other arms*, come into

53

collision with one another, the charge may often suffice for a decision. But where it is an affair of large masses, it will never be possible to dispense with the co-operation of firearms, and in most cases a combination of Cavalry combat, of dismounted fighting, and Artillery action, will ensue."

What lies behind this ambiguous language, which, remember, is the outcome of pure "speculation"? What principle is he trying to express? Let us proceed: "We must not conceal from ourselves the fact that in a future war it will be by no means always a matter of choice whether we will fight mounted or dismounted. *Rather by himself seizing the rifle will the opponent be able to compel us to adopt dismounted action.* On our manœuvre grounds the charge on horseback is always the order of the day, as against Artillery or machine-guns. The umpires continually allow such attacks to succeed, and the troops ride on as if nothing had happened. Equally fearless of consequences, do they expose themselves to rifle-fire; but there are no bullets. In real war it is different."

It is needless to point out that the words I have italicized destroy the whole case for the steel. They are an admission of the true principle that the rifle governs combat, whether the rifle is used by men with horses or men without horses. It is characteristic of the author that he cannot bring himself in this perilous context in set words to include Cavalry among those who "seize the rifle"; but the words themselves imply it, for we do not speak of Infantry "seizing the rifle." At a later point the author is a little bolder in the development of his meaning. "Our probable opponents, too, will certainly often advance dismounted. At all events, they are endeavouring to strengthen Cavalry divisions by cyclist battalions and Infantry, *and perhaps by Mounted Infantry,* and thereby already show a remarkable inclination to conduct

54

the fight, even of Cavalry, with the firearm, and only to use their horses as a means of mobility, as was the custom of the Boers in South Africa"—and he might, of course, add, of the British mounted riflemen and of the British Cavalry. If only the author, who has advanced thus far on the path of common sense, would just for one experimental moment assume an open mind on the question of the steel, assume that it may perhaps be not merely partially, but wholly obsolete, and study the Boer War with real care from that point of view! He evidently thinks there is something in this idea of using horses as a means of mobility and the rifle as the operative weapon. He expressly warns his Cavalry that their probable enemy is showing ominous signs of adopting this system, and that their adoption of it will force the German Cavalry to conform.

Now mark that magical word "mobility." It is the germ of a new idea, a faint effort to escape from the dupery of phrases. Hitherto he has always spoken of "dismounted action" as distinguished from "mounted" or "Cavalry" combat. These phrases are always used by Cavalry theorists. They take the place of argument, implying as they do that the use of the rifle reduces horsemen to the condition of Infantry, robbing them of mobility and all that glamour of dash and vigour which illuminates the mounted arm. The truth lies in the contrary direction. Without rifle power Cavalry lose all effective mobility. They can ride about *in vacuo*, so to speak; but directly they enter the zone of rifle-fire they are paralyzed, unless they can use their horses and their rifles in effective combination. Then they can do what they please. Then, if necessary, they can even charge mounted, though that function is no more inseparably associated with their action than the charge at the double is inseparably associated with the action of Infantry. But is it not somewhat ludicrous to describe as "dismounted action," in contradistinction to "mounted action," a charge which ends, as the Boer charges ended, within point-blank or decisive range of the enemy and culminates in a murderously decisive fire-attack?

The worst of it is that General von Bernhardi will not analyze his own warnings and suggestions and see what they really lead him to. He appears to see in these troublesome hordes of "cyclists" and "Mounted Infantry" who menace the old order of things and are forcing Cavalry to conform to fire by fire, only auxiliaries to the orthodox Cavalry. But Cavalry themselves carry the very weapon which is promoting the revolution; nor should any self-respecting, properly trained Cavalry need to fortify itself from these external sources. At a later stage I shall have to show, from our own Mounted Infantry Manual, how grotesque are the results obtained by the theoretical co-operation of steel and fire in two different types of troops.

And Sir John French? He has read these passages, and with one word of manly pride in the war experience of his own countrymen, home and colonial—experience bought at terrible cost, and not without bitter humiliation, in three years of "real war"—he could set the speculative German author right, illuminate the tortuous paths in which his reason strays. So far from taking this course, he proves himself more reactionary than his foreign colleague; for the reader will see at once that the spirit of passages quoted above is quite different from the spirit of Sir John French's Introduction. Von Bernhardi is alarmed by the prospect of meeting mounted riflemen who, as he knows and expressly admits, will impose upon his Cavalry fire-tactics of which they are contemptuously ignorant. He is alarmed at the prospect of the hostile Cavalry themselves "conducting the fight with the firearm." Sir John French, as I have shown, believes, and says, that our mounted riflemen and our

Cavalry, if they act as such, will "become the prey of the first foreign Cavalry they meet," running defenceless and helpless from the field. This is an example of the way in which Cavalry science proceeds, and it is a wonder that collaborators of the eminence of General von Bernhardi and General Sir John French do not see the humour of the thing, to use no stronger expression.

One watches with amusement the process by which the German author endeavours to soften the shock of the revelations he has just made to a Cavalry acutely sensitive about its ancient traditions. One of his plans, here and in many other parts of the book, is to play with the words "offence" and "defence," which, as I pointed out in commenting on Sir John French's Introduction, have such a strangely perverse influence on the Cavalry mind. "It lies deeply embedded in human nature," he says (p. 105), "that he who feels himself the weaker will act on the defensive"; and on the next page: "In general, it may be relied upon that defence will be carried out according to tactical defensive principles, and that with the firearm." Here is another example (italicized by me): "Mounted, the Cavalry knows only the charge, and has no defensive power, *a circumstance which strengthens it in carrying out its offensive principles by relieving its leader of the onus of choice*" (p. 113). Observe the idea suggested by these passages—namely, that the rifle is only a defensive weapon. Subtle indirect flattery of those who carry those terrible weapons of "offence," the lance and sword! But, alas! what he calls the "offensive spirit" must accept the terms imposed by the baser weapon. "It requires an enormous amount of moral strength," he says, "to maintain the *offensive spirit*, even after an unfavourable conflict, and continually to invoke the ultimate decision anew." There is a romantic atmosphere about this which might appeal to his hearers. Spent with charges, brilliant, but perhaps not wholly successful, they must resign themselves eventually to more sober, if less "knightly," methods. But this is not what he really means. He has just said that even in combats of the independent Cavalry the shock-charge will occur only "in exceptional cases." The probable opponents are to "*advance* dismounted"—in other words, to *attack* dismounted. This, he warns the Cavalry, will necessitate fire-action on their part. Why talk, then, about "relief from the onus of choice"? What is to happen when both sides are at grips on terms of fire? Is there a mutual deadlock, both remaining in "defence"? In that case there would be no battles and no necessity to go to war at all. Surely the common sense of the matter is that the rifle rules tactics, and that, *ceteris paribus*, the best riflemen will attack and win.

At heart the General believes this—his whole book is a witness to this fact—but how can he expect to get his beliefs accepted if he continually stultifies those beliefs by soothing ambiguities about the "offensive spirit"? Nor does he confine himself to ambiguity. Take a passage like this from p. 19, at the very outset of his chapter on "Reconnaissance, Screening, and Raids": "The very essence of Cavalry lies in the offensive. Mounted, it is incapable of tactical defence, *but in order to defend itself*, must surrender its real character as a mounted arm, and seize the rifle on foot." (The italics are mine.)

Conceive the mental chaos which can produce an expression of an opinion like this at the beginning of a work designed to reform the backward German Cavalry. Here, stated in formal, precise terms, is the very doctrine upon which that Cavalry works; which, as the author himself a hundred times assures us, is the source of all its "antiquated assumptions" and of its total unpreparedness for real war. The framers of the Regulations have only to point to this passage, and then, with perfect justice, to consign all the

General's tirades first to mockery and then to oblivion. Sir John French, again more reactionary than his German confrère, seizes on this passage, to the exclusion of all which contradict it, and triumphantly produces his own analogous formula. To neglect the steel, he says, is to "invert the rôle of Cavalry, and turn it into a defensive arm."

While Sir John French sticks to his point, and elaborates it even to the implicit denial of an offensive spirit to Infantry, General von Bernhardi is perfectly conscious of the absurdity of maintaining that it is only "in order to defend itself" that Cavalry "seize the rifle" on foot. We obtain, perhaps, the best insight into his method of reasoning in A II. ("Attack and Defence"). On p. 112 he says that Cavalry should "endeavour to preserve their mobility in the fight, and that mounted shock-action, *therefore*, should be regarded as its proper rôle in battle." This quotation is an excellent one for the advocates of the steel, but it would reduce to impotence any Cavalry which acted upon it. And we ask immediately, what is the sense of calling shock the "proper rôle" of Cavalry, when, according to the author himself, it is only to be used in exceptional cases, even in fights of the independent Cavalry, and when riflemen, who advance dismounted, can render it impracticable? Why not say at once that the proper or normal rôle of Cavalry is fire-action, and the exceptional or abnormal rôle shock-action?

The fallacy, of course, lies in the word I have italicized, "therefore," implying that mounted action and shock-action are synonymous, and that there is no mounted action without shock-action. It is natural enough that the author should turn his back on South Africa and Manchuria when he has to maintain such a proposition as this; but how does he reconcile it even with the facts of the American Civil War, which he holds up as the most valuable guide to modern Cavalry? Stuart, Sheridan, Wilson, and the other great leaders, would have laughed at it, and they used wretchedly imperfect firearms. They rode just as far and to just as good purpose whether they used the firearm or the steel, and they fought to win, with whatever weapon was the best weapon at the moment.

The General himself expresses the right idea when he says in another passage "that it is not a question whether Cavalrymen should fight mounted or dismounted, but whether they are prepared and determined to take their share in the decision of an encounter, and to employ the whole of their strength *and mobility* to that end." That is plain common sense; but how is he to get it acted upon by a Cavalry to whom the very idea is strange if he calls shock the "proper rôle" of Cavalry, and contrasts the "offensive spirit" inherent in it with the defensive use of the rifle?

Yet he redeems the rifle handsomely enough in numbers of other passages. "It must be kept in view," he says on p. 113, "that it is the *offensive* on foot that the Cavalry will require," and he condemns the Regulation which inculcates the opposite principle and deals with the fire-fight only as a method of action from which Cavalry "need not shrink." He shakes his head gravely over the ominous suggestion in the same Regulation that cyclists and Infantry in waggons are to be added to the Army Cavalry, in order, by fire, to "overcome local resistance." In a flash of insight he perceives the possibility of those heretical Mounted Infantry masquerading as the hostile Cavalry, and necessitating cyclists and Infantry in waggons to dislodge them before the "knightly combats" can be brought about. "It is a matter of significance," he solemnly observes, "that Infantry in waggons may be detailed to accompany the strategic Army Cavalry." There will soon be a demand, he prophesies, "for Infantry from the Army Cavalry when there is any question of a serious attack on foot, and herewith the free action of the Cavalry will be limited once and for all." Is there no lesson from South Africa here?

The fact is that the kind of thing he fears happened from the first, and continued to happen until the Cavalry abandoned steel weapons and became mounted riflemen. During the first year of the war there was no independent Cavalry force operating strategically without the assistance of mounted riflemen. There could not have been, because the fire-power of the Cavalry was insufficient, and there is and can be no independence in modern war without a high degree of fire-power. Cavalry leaders usually asked also for the tactical assistance of mounted riflemen. The theory, surviving even now in the current manuals, was that those troops were to form a "pivot" for the shock-action of Cavalry. The theory, of course, was exploded from the first, and sometimes the mounted riflemen became the most effective and mobile portion of the composite force. Mounted riflemen were a truly independent Arm. They never asked for the assistance of Cavalry on the ground that Cavalry carried steel weapons. The rifle was all they cared about, and they had good rifles of their own, while the Cavalry had bad carbines. The only big independent Cavalry enterprise during the first year of the war—the divisional march across the Eastern Transvaal in October, 1900—was a fiasco. The Cavalry formed but an escort to their own transport, and developed no offensive power.

Von Bernhardi, just now thoroughly in his fire-mood, strongly condemns the theory of dependence on other Arms, which will "tie the Cavalry" to the very troops from which they expect support. "The army Cavalry, then, can only preserve its independence if it can rely upon its own strength even in an attack on foot." He goes on to criticize Regulation No. 456, which lays down that "Cavalry must endeavour to bring dismounted attacks to a conclusion with the utmost rapidity, so that they may regain their mobility at the earliest possible moment." The regulation, which has its counterpart in the British Manual, indeed, is laughable to anyone who has seen modern war. Troopers who spend 90 per cent. of their time on exercises with the steel will necessarily attack badly, clumsily, and slowly on foot, and it is a cruel jest to tell them to attack quickly and brilliantly. In a fire-contest the best riflemen will attack the quickest and do the best.

But the General wastes his breath in scolding the Regulations. They are more logical than he is, because they do not seriously contemplate this derogatory work of fire. He says, indeed, that unnaturally accelerated attacks on foot by men who do not know how to attack on foot only succeed in peace, and will "lead inevitably to defeat in war," and that to set a time limit to a fire-attack is absurd; but by interspersing qualifying phrases about loss of mobility and loss of time he himself nullifies his own warnings. "The result of an attack on foot," he says (p. 116), "must, of course, justify the lives expended and the time occupied, *which must both be regarded as lost in estimating the further operative value of the force."* Men who read that will say: "Why waste time at all, then?" It is in flagrant contradiction, of course, with his previously expressed principle that hostile fire imposes fire-action on Cavalry; that there is no choice; that, whether they like it or not, they *must* engage in this rôle, which, nevertheless, is not their "proper rôle." The clue to the confusion, as always, is his view, founded on mere word-play, that mounted action is unthinkable without shock with steel weapons.

At the end of this section on "Attack and Defence" he continues to play into the hands of the framers of the Regulations which he denounces. Here is an immortal phrase: "The same holds good of the defence. *Cavalry will only undertake this when absolutely obliged.*" This is the kind of maxim which one finds scattered broadcast through Cavalry literature—as if there could be any offence without defence, between or against whatever classes of soldiers. Fancy telling Infantry or Artillery in so many words that they should only undertake defence when absolutely obliged! And yet they are just as much offensive Arms as Cavalry, and by the light of historical facts during the last century a great deal more so.

I need not go into the reason again. The General is in his steel-mood, and is unconsciously limiting offence to the steel weapons. The next instant he is in his fire-mood, pointing out that, however much Cavalry in defence may yearn once more for "free movement" (he means shock), they must be prepared on occasion to defend themselves—*i.e.*, with fire— to the last man. And he very aptly illustrates from the Manchurian War (which at an earlier point he had said to be without interest for Cavalry), pointing to the stubborn defence of Sandepu by a Japanese Cavalry Brigade. We cannot help wishing that Sir John French would quote and confirm an opinion like this, flatly contradicted though it is a little later,[2] and use his influence to erase from our own Cavalry Manual (p. 215) that disastrous injunction that the defences of a position which Cavalry have to hold should be "limited to those of the simplest kind."

If the words "attack" and "defence" have a fatal fascination for both the German and the British authors, General von Bernhardi is equally influenced by another verbal formula, and that is "the combination of Cavalry combat" (or, what is the same thing to him, mounted combat—that is, shock-combat) "with dismounted fighting." "The rôle of Cavalry in the fight will then apparently consist," he says on page 106, "of a combination of the various methods of fighting." It is a tempting formula, tempting by its very vagueness, and

63

calculated on that account to appeal, perhaps, to the less hopelessly conservative German Cavalry officers; but it remains throughout his book literally a formula. How the thing is to be done in practice, how shock is to be "combined" with fire, he never attempts, even from a speculative point of view, to explain. It may sound perhaps easy enough. In the war of 1861-1865, which he professes to take as his model, it undoubtedly was possible, if by no means easy. But times have changed. The modern rifle, whose profound influence on combat he admits, has made impossible the old formations. In his own phrase, it has revolutionized war. It enforces a degree of extension which renders impracticable those sudden transformations to close mass which alone can lead to shock, while the zone of danger it creates is so far-reaching that these mass formations on horseback cannot subsist. The conditions which used to permit leaders to resolve on shock have vanished. The fire-zone used to be so limited that bodies of Cavalry could hang on its outer limit, and seize the rare opportunities which might arise for a short gallop ending in shock. Now we have to deal with artillery and rifles of immense range and deadliness. And if by a miracle you do get into close quarters in your mass formation, you find— crowning disillusionment!—nothing solid on which to exert shock. You used to find it a century ago, because men used to fight in close order, but science has altered that. However, that point does not immediately arise from the question of "combination." The narrow issue there is how to effect the transition from fire to shock, and there is not a word in this volume to elucidate the point. There is not a word in our own Cavalry Manual. The thing has never been done in modern war. The combination of shock and fire tactics is an academical speculation. What we know is that shock has failed, and that the open-order rifle-charge, which has superseded the shock-charge, is evolved naturally from the fire-fight. You must, in the words of Lord Roberts, fight up to the charge, if charge there be; but you can win, as Infantry can win, without any mounted charge at all.

FOOTNOTES:

[2] See *infra*, pp. 122-123.

CHAPTER V

TACTICS AGAINST THE VARIOUS ARMS

I.—THE PURELY CAVALRY FIGHT.

("Das rein reiterliche Gefecht.")

THESE two sections which I have been criticizing will give the reader a general idea of the way in which von Bernhardi regards the action of Cavalry in modern war, and of the perplexities which beset him through mingling of the old philosophy and the new. Let us follow him through subsequent sections of head B ("Action of Cavalry"). The third section deals with "Cavalry in combat against the various Arms, mounted and dismounted," and he first deals with what he calls the "purely Cavalry fight," which he now assumes to be a fight with the steel against other Cavalry. We must remember that if either side elects to use the rifle; or if the ground is unsuitable (and on page 201 he argues at length that "possible European theatres of war are but little suitable for charges," and that suitable areas are only found in peace by deliberate selection); or if either side, from numerical weakness or choice, is acting on the "defensive" (defence with the steel being *ex hypothesi* impossible), this steel combat will not take place.

Under the circumstances it seems scarcely worth while to talk about it, but let us waive that objection. We at once become impressed with a very remarkable fact—namely, that after all the centuries, extending far back into the mists of time, during which the mounted steel-combat has been used, its most learned and enthusiastic advocates cannot at this day agree upon the elementary rules for its conduct. Observe that I am excluding the modifications caused by missile weapons. Following the author, I am assuming a combat between two bodies of Cavalry who decline to use their firearms, and mutually agree to collide with steel weapons on horseback, outside the zone of fire, on a piece of level ground without physical obstruction. For this type of combat the conditions are the same as in the year one. The three factors—horse, man, and steel weapon—have undergone no appreciable change, and by this time the rules ought to be fixed. Yet we find the General at once falling into tirades against erroneous systems, and bitterly denouncing the Regulations of his own Army.

"The lance," we learn on page 267, "is the Cavalryman's most important weapon," yet the drill laid down for the lance the author declares to be worthless. "No one would fight in this manner in war; how this is to be done our men are not really taught." What a confession after all these ages, from the Crusades onwards! And if the lance is really the most important weapon, and if Sir John French really believes, as he says he believes, in the infallibility of General von Bernhardi, why has he not seen to it that all British Cavalry regiments are armed with lances? It would seem to be mad folly to permit our Hussars to go into battle destitute of their "most important weapon." But let us look a little closer into the characteristics of this terrible weapon. On page 175 we learn that "in the close turmoil of the fight it is very difficult to handle with success, besides which it easily becomes unserviceable on striking an object too heavily. Should it pierce a body at the full speed of a horse's gallop, it will generally bend on being drawn out (if, indeed, the rider in his haste extricates it at all), and then becomes unserviceable." So there must be a sword also, which is to be drawn, apparently, on the instant after the impalement of the first hostile horseman. Our own authorities take a brighter view. In their Manual the trooper is bidden to impale the foe through and through with his lance, but he is to "withdraw it with ease from the object into which it has been driven." On the other hand, the object in question is to be represented in peace by a sack filled with chopped hay or a clay dummy, neither of them objects of a texture quite adequate to the purpose (see "Cavalry Training," pp. 309-310).

It is almost cruel to lift the veil from these domestic mysteries and differences, and, indeed, I am almost afraid my readers will suspect me of quoting, not from eulogies, but from skits on the *arme blanche*. But the words are there for anyone who cares to look them up, and I ask, is not it almost inconceivable that serious soldiers in the year of grace 1911, when war is a really serious matter of scientific weapons, should solemnly call a weapon with such characteristics the most important weapon of the Cavalryman? Needless to say, the author himself refutes his own proposition in a hundred passages of this very work. But Sir John French ignores those passages, and in his own Introduction pens a warm defence of the lance; though whether he believes in the "pin-prick policy" which the German authority seems to advocate, or in the plan of "striking the object heavily" at all costs, he does not inform us. After all, it matters little. The taxpayer need not quail at the expense of providing fresh lances to every regiment after every charge. The rest of the world looks on with languid interest while the Cavalry authorities carry on their solemn controversies as to the relative merits of steel weapons used from horseback. Even in the Franco-German War the killing effect of lances and swords was negligible. Six Germans were killed by the sabre, and perhaps as many by the lance. Of the total of 218 German casualties from the sabre and clubbed musket, 138 were in the Cavalry, whose total losses by fire and steel combined were 2,236. In the great civilized wars since the invention of the smokeless magazine rifle the casualties from lance and sword have reached vanishing-point.

But if lances and swords are harmless to the enemy, they are emphatically harmful to those who carry them. They not only inspire the wrong spirit, but they mean extra weight and additional visibility. Sir John French (p. xvi) cheerfully defies physical laws. He scouts the idea that "a thin bamboo pole will reveal the position of a mounted man to the enemy." That is one of the fond illusions of peace. And in peace even a short-sighted layman could prove the contrary by ocular demonstration, and digest the moral, too, by watching Lancers operating among the lanes and hedges of England. In war there are field-glasses—and bullets.

It is the same with tactics as with weapons. The German author is for the knee-to-knee riding of Frederick the Great, as opposed to the looser stirrup-to-stirrup riding which has been introduced because "the modern firearm obliges us to take refuge in broken country, where the closest touch cannot always be kept." A pretty sound reason, we should imagine, but the General will have none of it, and I think this passage is the only one in the book where he disagrees with the Regulations in the matter of a concession to the modern rifle. Generally it is the other way, and, indeed, it is a most bizarre paradox to hear him calling upon the shades of "Frederick the Great, Seydlitz, and the prominent Napoleonic leaders," after saying at the beginning of the book that the wars of these heroes "presented a total absence of analogy" to modern Cavalry students. Reverting suddenly to common sense, he goes on to denounce the rally from the mêlée, which all Cavalry, including our own, assiduously practise in peace. The motive for this wonderful manœuvre is "that troops may quickly be got in hand ready to be led against a fresh foe." "It is astounding," he complains, "that we should give way to such self-deception." Rallies are "delightfully easy in peace," but an "absolute impossibility in war."

The troops who have charged are apparently to be useless for any purpose whatever for an indefinite period, and strong supporting squadrons immediately behind them must carry on the fight. But the new Regulations do not allow for these supports. What do they enjoin? We are not told here, and have to look in another part of the book under "Depth and Echelon" (p. 221 *et seq.*), when, calling once more upon Frederick the Great and Napoleon, he attacks in unmeasured terms, as the offspring of mere "peace requirements," the German system of echelon formation, which leads to "tactical orgies" at manœuvres. Echelon apparently is designed to permit of easy changes of front, but in war the opportunity for such changes "never—literally never—occurs." And yet somehow we sympathize with the framers of the Regulations. Read their inimitable disquisition on echelon, quoted as a footnote on page 224. "In the collisions of Cavalry" there is going to be "uncertainty as to the strength and intentions of the enemy." But Cavalry acting against Cavalry (supposing, we wonder, they turn out *not* to be Cavalry?) never demean themselves by dismounting to reconnoitre. They reconnoitre for one another in mass, and gain the necessary "flexibility" by echelon—if need be, by a double echelon. When they find the enemy, they can at the last moment, if necessary, change front completely, and have at them. "If this did occur," says the General, "it would presuppose the entire failure of reconnaissance, and the corresponding incapacity of the leader." He proceeds to a pitiless exposure of the puerilities and unrealities of the system; but, to tell the truth, the exposure excites only a feeble interest. Insensibly he trenches on the realms of fire, and immediately stultifies his own appeals to Frederick the Great and Napoleon. After pages of obscure lucubration about Cavalry combat, he suddenly envisages (p. 230) what is, of course, the invariable case, when "total uncertainty prevails as to whether the combat will be carried out mounted or dismounted," and says that in such cases there can be no "stereotyped tactical formations either of units or of smaller bodies within them." "Cadit quæstio," we exclaim, with relief. Why appeal to Frederick the Great?

In "Formations for Movement" (pp. 232-238) he continues his unconscious *reductio ad absurdum* of shock. "Movements in such close formation right up to the moment of deployment" (and he describes those enjoined by the Regulations) "cannot go unpunished upon a modern battle-field." The Regulations "cannot be regarded as practical," and are "pretexts for hidebound drill enthusiasts." It is all very well, but these hidebound gentlemen are perfectly right in their own way. They are following his own models, Frederick the Great and Napoleon, in whose days such movements were perfectly possible. They *believe* in shock and minimize fire, and their Regulations, if unpractical, are at least logical.

II. — THE CHARGE UPON INFANTRY.

So much for the "purely Cavalry fight." We come on page 128 to the mounted charge upon dismounted riflemen, whom, in the manner usual with Cavalry writers, he assumes to be Infantry, though it is obvious, of course, that they may be unconventional Cavalry, who, from a sense of fun or a sane instinct for fighting, have determined to play a practical joke on devotees of the pure faith. Here both he

71

and the Regulations are up to a certain point in harmony with one another. As a concession to modern conditions, the charge is to be in *extended order*. Here the General has changed his views since writing "Cavalry in Future Wars." There the principles of Frederick the Great were supreme in all charges, with just a faint concession towards a "loosening of the files" in a charge against Infantry. Now "wide intervals" are to be employed. Sir John French ignores the change of view on an absolutely vital point of tactics, but allows us to infer that he, one of the very men who saw the imperative necessity for the new view, favours the old view; for he described von Bernhardi's first book as absolutely complete and faultless. To return, however, to the German author. It is amazing that, having reached this point, he should not trouble to investigate the phenomena of modern war with a view to finding out what actually happens in an extended change of this sort. He writes in the clouds, just as though there were not a mass of experience bearing on the point.

The experience, which a child can understand, amounts to this: If you extend, and, *a fortiori*, if your enemy is extended also, you lose all hope of "shock," that is, of physical impact; and with the loss of this impact you lose the fundamental condition precedent to the successful use of steel weapons on horseback—the condition which Frederick the Great's leaders had, but which ours have not. You also lose momentum, speed, because the modern rifle, by immensely widening the bullet-swept zone, necessitates a far longer gallop for the charging force. The German Regulations realize this, for they enjoin a slower pace, expressly on the ground that "impact" is not to be aimed at. Very well: no shock; comparatively low speed. What is going to happen? Your steel charge is useless. Individual troopers, bound by their code of honour to remain in the saddle, and pitted against individual riflemen on foot, are helpless, an object of derision to gods and men. Our own Infantry Manual openly treats them as helpless and negligible, and in a few curt lines gives directions, proved in war to be sound, for the event of such a charge, should it take place.

But, in fact, it does not take place. Our Cavalry in South Africa had literally thousands of chances of making such charges, supposing that they were feasible. But they were not; instinctively the leaders felt that they were not, and ceased to think of making them. At the time when, if ever, any given leader should have made up his mind to charge, he was, unfortunately, as a general rule, in that condition of painful "uncertainty as to the strength and intentions of the enemy," to which the German Regulations allude. He could not, in the German fashion, ride about in mass to reconnoitre, because the Boers, perversely refusing to believe in the tactics of Frederick the Great, did not co-operate in the game. He had, therefore, the choice between idleness and fire-action. He chose fire-action, and once engaged in fire-action, he found that he had to stick to it. It was physically impossible to "combine" fire-action and steel-action, even if there had been an opening for steel-action, which there was not. That is the whole story, and Sir John French, if he chose, could tell General von Bernhardi all about it.

I believe Sir John French himself never saw a Boer or British mounted riflemen's charge, but he ought to know the evidence on the point; it is extensive and precise.[3] It goes to show that it is sometimes possible, even against the modern rifle, to charge in widely extended order, even at a canter, and even into close quarters, on horseback; but it can be done only by fighting up to the charge in the normal way of fire-action, and by casting to the winds the ancient notion that it is beneath a trooper to dismount. Sooner or later he has *got* to dismount, so as to use effective aimed fire against the riflemen opposed to him. They will not mind his sword, whose range is a couple of yards, while their weapon is of any range you please, and squirts bullets like a hose.

Frederick the Great's Infantry firearm was another matter. Even in 1861-1865, as von Bernhardi would discover if he cared to look close enough into his own chosen war, steel-charges by Cavalry against Infantry eventually became extinct. The Confederate Infantry used to jeer at the futile efforts of the Federal Cavalry.

Needless to say, the German Regulations only touch the fringe of what is practicable. It is only the leading line, they lay down, and not necessarily the whole even of that, which is to adopt wide intervals. Von Bernhardi easily shows the folly of these half-measures, and of the "arbitrary assumption that a line of Cavalry 1,500 or 2,000 yards wide can cross a mile of country stirrup to stirrup at the regulation pace of the charge" (p. 128).

III.—THE DISMOUNTED ATTACK BY CAVALRY.

We pass to the dismounted attack by Cavalry, and the reader will realize now, if he has not before, that it is due to unfamiliarity with the technique and true possibilities of fire-action that the General clings to the discredited tactics of Frederick the Great in defiance of his professed enthusiasm for the rifle. For the dismounted attack by Cavalry, "the principles," he says, "are the same as for an attack by Infantry" (p. 133). But the led horses render the business "considerably more difficult." "There is also a certain difference according as the opponent is Cavalry or Infantry"; for in the former case he may charge your led horses. It is here and in the pages which follow that the reader can get the clearest insight into the mental attitude of Cavalrymen towards that arbiter of modern war, the rifle.

All turns on the magical word "Cavalry," which derives its

significance from the *arme blanche*. Those weapons give Cavalry their "proper rôle." If under stress of fire they "abandon" this rôle, they become Infantry; but they are worse off than Infantry, because they are embarrassed by their led horses, which present difficulties from which Infantry are free. The horse becomes a danger and an encumbrance, just as Sir John French tacitly assumes it to become, when he says that mounted riflemen always flee defenceless before good Cavalry, while Infantry show "tenacity and stiffness." No wonder, then, that Cavalrymen grow indignant at the criticism of their steel weapons. It is bad enough to be converted into a hybrid between good Cavalry and bad Infantry, but it is worse still to undergo a metamorphosis into a pure type of bad Infantry, that is, into mounted riflemen.

If we once grasp this point of view, we bring light into this tangled controversy, and we can bring into sharp contrast the rational point of view, as the facts of war demonstrate it. We perceive instantly the falsity of the antithesis between the weapon and the horse. The mounted rifleman is a foot rifleman plus a horse, and the horse is not an embarrassing encumbrance, but a source of enhanced power. It is the intrusion of the steel weapons, not the intrusion of the horses, which introduces "difficulties." Witness von Bernhardi's own scathing exposure of the German Regulations for combat with the steel.

Space forbids me to follow him far into his remarks upon his bugbear, the led horses. There are probably about 150,000 persons now living who, by war experience, know more than he does about this purely technical question; yet he spins feverish dreams about it out of his own brain, without a glance at the rich and varied material provided by three years of war in South Africa; without a glance at Manchuria, where the Japanese Cavalry converted themselves into excellent mounted riflemen; without a glance even at the American methods of 1861-1865, where the problems that worry him were successfully solved. As usual, he has no difficulty in exposing the absurdities of the Regulations, but his own comments and suggestions are sometimes even less admissible. Behind the incubus of the horse we perceive that additional incubus, the lance. He pictures the unhappy horse-holders wrestling ("a practical impossibility") with armfuls of lances, as the Regulations bid them (p. 137), and concludes that if you are to make these men guardians, not only of the horses, but of these precious but exacting impedimenta, it will not do to detail only one man out of four to act as horseholder. On the other hand, if you detach more, you weaken the firing line so much that the whole business becomes scarcely worth while. And yet, if you don't weaken the firing line, how are you to guard the led horses against attack from some other quarter? They, it appears, must have a complete firing line of their own. But, disregarding this necessity, the Regulations contemplate reinforcing the main firing-line from the horse-holders (p. 139), so making the armfuls of lances still bigger. And then what is to happen if, in a "real fight," the brigade wants to advance and the Brigadier is told it can't, because some of the horse-holders are fighting, and the lance-encumbered remnant cannot move? And so on. He seems, so far as I understand him, eventually to throw up in despair the problem of keeping the led horses "mobile," and to fall back on the plan of "immobility," a plan which he himself in several passages admits can be used only when there is no likelihood whatever of any sudden call upon the led horses either for advance or retreat. If the Regulations, as he says, are "not suitable for real war," neither is his counsel of despair. The chapter is quite enough to cure the most liberal-minded Cavalryman of his last lingering inclination towards fire-action, even though he is told that fire-action

76

must be used in all but "exceptional cases." "Abandon my proper rôle for this?" he might answer. "No. My proper rôle is good enough for me, as it was good enough for Frederick the Great."

There is worse to come; but let me comment here upon the astounding fact that Sir John French should regard chapters like this as sound instruction for war. Our Cavalry profess, at any rate, to have now solved the lance-problem during fire-action by their latest method of carrying the lance. But that is a minor point. It is the ignorance of, and pessimism towards, fire-action, as disclosed in this and subsequent chapters, which ought chiefly to strike English readers. And all Sir John French has to say is that "we expose our ignorance and conceit" in accepting the teaching of our own war experience, and that our duty is to assimilate the best foreign customs.

FOOTNOTES:

[3] See "War and the *Arme Blanche,*" Chapter XI.

CHAPTER VI

THE FIGHT OF THE INDEPENDENT CAVALRY

I. — GERMAN VIEWS.

FROM his general remarks on the action of Cavalry, mounted or dismounted, against the various Arms, mounted or dismounted, the author passes to "IV.—The Fight of the Independent Cavalry" (p. 141), and the reader almost at once finds himself straying in a fog caused by the author's refusal to face straightforwardly the simple dominant fact that "Cavalry" are also riflemen. What does "Independent" mean?

One would naturally assume it to mean what it means in our own Cavalry's phraseology, the "strategical" Cavalry which operates on a self-supporting independent basis, as distinguished from the divisional Cavalry, which is attached to, and dependent on, the various Infantry divisions. And this is the signification which the author gives to it in the opening words of the chapter. "Such fights," he says, "will occur during the offensive reconnaissance of the Cavalry, in screening, and in enterprises against the enemy's communication and lines of approach" (that is, in raids), functions which are classified in the same order in the early part of the book as the normal functions of the Independent Cavalry, operating, in the first instance at any rate, against a hostile Independent Cavalry of the same stamp and vested with corresponding functions. We expect, accordingly, to hear a great deal about the "purely Cavalry fight," or shock-combat; but, to our bewilderment, after less than a page of exceedingly obscure reference to the "exceptional cases," where, owing to the absence of "other arms," such combats occur, the author proceeds to examine what he evidently regards as the normal case, "when the co-operation of other arms can seriously be counted on," and the whole of the forty-eight pages which follow implicitly assume that other Arms, whether in the shape of Artillery, Infantry, cyclists, or what he vaguely calls "partisans," are present. Artillery alone are enough, he says, to scatter to the winds "purely Cavalry tactical principles," and "to set the stamp of fire upon the development of the fight" (p. 144). The unfortunate Cavalry subaltern must feel the ground sinking under his feet. The book he is studying, "Cavalry in War and Peace," is a treatise for Cavalry on purely Cavalry tactical principles, and yet these principles cease to exist if even Artillery are on the scene, as in most normal cases it is assumed to be on the scene. Both in Germany and in England Horse Artillery is a recognized and integral part of the Independent Cavalry force whose functions the author is now considering. What is more, rifles are an invariable factor in the same force, German or English, or, indeed, in any force of Cavalry of whatever size, and however engaged, because they are carried by the Cavalry troopers themselves. And rifles, as the author will soon explain, make still worse havoc of purely Cavalry tactical principles. In other words, there *are* no such principles.

We may cut the matter short by merely advising the reader to solve his perplexities in the succeeding chapters by substituting for the word "Cavalry," whenever it occurs, the words "mounted riflemen," which, steel weapons apart, are what Cavalry are. There he will have a key to most of the contradictions and ambiguities, and can form his own opinion on the lucidity and force of the injunctions laid down. The truth is that the General, in speaking of "other arms," really means not only other Arms of the service (*i.e.*, Infantry and Artillery), but other *weapons*, as distinguished from lances and swords, carried by Cavalry themselves— that is, *rifles*.

Armed with this clue, let us begin.

We must classify, says the author, with his critical eye on the Regulations, "for if we take all the various principles evolved from different tactical situations, and jumble them illogically together, or discuss them from points of view which are not closely based on the probable happenings of reality, we run a danger of confusing the judgment instead of clearing it." He proceeds himself to involve our judgments in irremediable confusion.

First of all, fights, according to the old phrase, are either offensive or defensive. Offensive fights are of two sorts: "battles of encounter," where the "enemy is also pressing forward," and "attacks against localities or positions."

Defensive fights are of only one main character: they require the defence of localities, positions, and defiles. Then, in quite a separate category, comes a third class of fights—namely, "surprises, which merit separate consideration"—a consideration, it may be noted, that they never get. The author forgets all about them. It matters little. His classification as it stands is as far removed from the "happenings of reality" as any classification could be; and to divorce surprise, generally supposed to be the soul of all mounted action (because horses mean high mobility) from "battles of encounter," "attacks on localities," and other sorts of fights, is only to supply the crowning element of unreality. It must be remembered that his most comprehensive classification (of which the above is a subdivision) distinguishes between "the fight of the Independent Cavalry" and the "action of Cavalry in battle," by which latter phrase he means the great battle of all Arms; and that battle, he has said, is "always of a pre-arranged nature"—that is, lacking in opportunities for surprise. One would have imagined, therefore, that if he wanted an antithesis between surprise and something else, he would oppose the pre-arranged battle to the fight of the Independent Cavalry. Not so. "Surprises" are left out in the cold and eventually forgotten.

And what of these other sorts of fights defined under their various heads? Perhaps I had better take them in detail, rather than attempt a general diagnosis.

What is the battle of encounter? I have collected all the allusions I can find to this battle, in the hope of supplying an intelligible definition, but have to admit failure. On page 102 it is distinguished from an "arranged affair," a distinction which in peace suggests those carefully-planned "knightly combats" on level pieces of ground, but which in war does not carry us very far. On page 147, however, the special case of a battle of encounter where "an opponent is unexpectedly met with," receives separate consideration. On page 142 it seems to denote the case "where the enemy is also pressing forward," again a somewhat nebulous description, for it is the common way of enemies to press forward. On page 143 one thinks for a moment that it is to be confined to "lesser bodies of Cavalry, unaccompanied by other arms"; but one speedily finds allusion to "larger bodies of Cavalry, accompanied by a proportion of other arms," and the co-operation of other arms becomes the predominant feature of the whole discussion. Yet on page 194, in discussing the action of the army Cavalry on the flank of a great battle, the author speaks of a battle of encounter between the rival Cavalry masses, as though this type of fight were confined to Cavalry. Again, on page 154 it is held to include the passage of defiles, though the defence of defiles, a function which is the necessary counterpart of the passage of defiles, is, as we have seen, regarded as belonging to a separate type of combat.

We have noted also the distinction between the battles of encounter and "attacks of localities," and between these latter and the defence of localities (as though there were any antithesis between an encounter on the one hand and an attack or defence on the other!). But what is a "locality," an attack on which is distinguished from a battle of encounter? Here is a fresh mystery. A "locality," on page 174, is distinguished from a "prepared position," which Cavalry, he says here, are never to attack or defend,[4] and it appears, in fact, to be simply a place on which troops are (a "place within the meaning of the Act," we cannot help exclaiming). In the first words of the section on "Attack of Localities" this attack is explained as one upon "an enemy who takes up a defensive attitude."

If, therefore, in a battle of encounter, when both sides are "pressing forward," one side or the other halts temporarily (without preparing or entrenching a position), the other side is in the position of attacking a locality; and if the former party repulses the attack and resumes its advance, then the position is reversed. Or if there is a temporary equilibrium in the fight, when neither party can make headway, then both are attacking and both are defending localities. But some such phenomena as these are common to all combats. Where, then, is the battle of encounter?

This is no idle question, and these are no hair-splitting criticisms, because the rules are held to differ in important respects in these various types of combats. In the battle of encounter there are some exceedingly dim indications of an opening for the steel, but an attack upon a "locality" "*can obviously only be carried out dismounted*" (p. 165). Pass by the old fallacious antagonism between mounted action and rifle action, and regard the essence of this proposition. Once again you have the refutation of the steel theory. The sentence means "fire governs combat." He who fires compels his enemy to accept combat on terms of fire.

But "Where am I?" the harassed student may exclaim. "What of these steel-charges against extended Infantry (and, by inference, against dismounted Cavalry), whose fire enforced extension in the attacking Cavalry?" Well, let him read on. There is hope yet. For immediately after saying that an attack upon an enemy who takes up a defensive attitude can obviously only be carried out dismounted, he adds the sinister words: "It must be a matter, therefore, for serious consideration, whether such an operation shall be undertaken or not." The truth is that he has suddenly remembered those tiresome led horses. "There must be considerable numerical superiority to insure success." There must be a dismounted reserve for fire purposes, and a mounted reserve to secure the safety of the led horses, and "for reconnaissance and for operating against the enemy's flank and rear"; and then follows an acrimonious wrangle with the Regulations on the question of making one reserve, and that mounted, perform incompatible and contradictory functions. But, as usual, our sympathies are with the Regulations.

"Should the Cavalry commander not have at his disposal sufficient force to meet all these demands," says the General, "he will be generally better advised to abstain from the attack and to carry out his mission in some other manner...." "It is only when conscious of great moral and tactical superiority, or when there is any prospect of surprising the enemy, that an attack should be dared without the necessary numerical preponderance" (p. 166). In other words, after his *reductio ad absurdum* of the steel, the writer in the next breath proceeds to an equally conclusive *reductio ad absurdum* of the rifle. Any Cavalry leader who acted on the General's principles would be instantly sent home in disgrace. According to these principles, numerically equal bodies of Cavalry cannot fight one another at all unless in those "exceptional cases" where the ground is favourable for the "purely Cavalry fight," when there are no other Arms to complicate the situation, and where neither side even for a moment "takes up a defensive attitude" for any purpose whatever. If any one of these conditions is unsatisfied, the numerically equal forces are mutually paralyzed, and each must seek to "carry out its mission in some other manner." But, alas! by hypothesis there is no other manner. "The attack obviously can only be made dismounted." Presumably, then, these Cavalries are to do nothing at all in modern war.

I am not making an unfair use of isolated passages. In later portions of his work the General frequently repeats his warnings against fire-action without great numerical and moral superiority, though not, perhaps, so frequently and emphatically as he inveighs against impracticable shock-action. Under "VIII.—The Various Units in the Fight" (p. 239), we learn that a "squadron is generally too weak to carry out an offensive fight on foot." By the time you have abstracted horse-holders, "mounted and dismounted reserves," and "patrols and sentries," there is nothing left with which to fight. Similarly, a squadron must never "undertake a defensive fight on foot unless absolutely necessary, or when the led horses can be disposed in a safe place in the neighbourhood, where the flanks cannot be turned, or where the arrival of reinforcements can be relied on." Observe that there is no limitation here as to the strength of the enemy, no demand for numerical or moral superiority. The rule is almost absolute. A squadron can only charge on horseback. So that in average enclosed country, where charges cannot be arranged, two opposed squadrons must maintain a masterly inactivity. We think of the 74 isolated "Zarps" at Bergendal in their desperate defence against enormous odds, and of the 150 Griqualanders who defied a division of Cavalry for a whole day at Dronfield.

But the General is far from stopping with the squadron. "The *regiment* will seldom be called upon to fight independently, but will operate in more or less close co-operation with other troops." It can act dismounted, but only "against weaker hostile detachments." In defence, however, it is "formidable," because—strange reason—it can detach two whole squadrons to guard the led horses! Well, it is no wonder that the author neglects and discourages the study of modern war. Supposing De Wet, for example, had acted on his principles! His brilliant intervention at Paardeberg was made with 350 men. Or go to Manchuria. Naganuma's masterly raid of January to February, 1905, when he rode round the Russian army and blew up the great bridge of Hsin-kai-ho, was made with 172 Cavalrymen, who acted throughout solely by fire, and would have been impotent without it. The author professes to admire the exploits of the Americans in 1861-1865. What does he suppose their Cavalry leaders would have thought of his theories?

The brigade of two regiments, we learn next, is almost as feeble a unit as a regiment. "It cannot," he says vaguely, "engage an opponent of any strength who may have to be dealt with by mounted or dismounted action, or the two in combination." "In view of its small offensive power, it will run a great risk of suffering defeat, *especially when dismounted*." In defence, "if the led horses do not require too large an escort," etc., it "may be an important factor of strength."

The division of six regiments (of 400 men per regiment) is a somewhat more useful unit. "If its full strength can be employed in the charge," it "represents, even against troops using the rifle" (what troops? of what strength?), "a considerable fighting power." Nevertheless, it can attack "only weak detachments with a prospect of success." "The resistance of a body of equal strength" (a body of what? how composed?) "when circumstances demand a dismounted attack can never be overcome." Mounted, however, and "charging in close formation," it can attack even a stronger enemy (what sort of enemy?), "regardless of consequences."

Finally, a corps of two divisions "can aim at decisive results," and, alone of all units, can engage in "independent strategic missions," which we may suppose, without further explanation, to mean raids. But in these "fire-power is an important factor," and it is hinted that even the corps will not have enough fire-power.

The General complains that his writings "fall on barren soil." Well they may. Antiquated as the methods of the German Cavalry are, they at any rate intend to fight. A Cavalry educated on the maxims of the author might as well be left at home.

And this is the author that Sir John French, who knows what our own mounted riflemen did in South Africa, holds up as a model to our Cavalry. He has not one word of criticism, not a single reservation, to make on any of the passages I have quoted. On the contrary, he tells our men, in general terms, that it is all true, and implies that the greatest of his compatriot soldiers, Lord Roberts, makes "appeals from vanity to ignorance." A perusal of this chapter, and of Sir John French's effusive eulogy, ought to make every British soldier, home or colonial, indignant.

Its conclusion (pp. 245-246) is not the least remarkable part of it. "It will seldom be possible," says the General, conscious, seemingly, that his counsels have not been vividly luminous, "and generally unnecessary to undertake or carry out the very best course of action, for we may certainly count on numerous errors and vacillations on the part of the enemy, *especially in the case of Cavalry warfare.*" Well, we may heartily endorse the words I have italicized.

Then, as a last desperate resort, come high-sounding generalities. "The indomitable will to conquer carries with it a considerable guarantee of success ... and the offensive is the weapon with which he [the Cavalry leader] can best enforce his will." Offensive!

The reader may infer from the passages I have quoted that it is not necessary to examine in close detail the General's instructions for the "battle of encounter" and the "attack of localities." He will trip at every ambiguous sentence, baffled by contradictions or qualifications somewhere else, and

86

perpetually befogged either by the vague word "enemy" or the implied distinction between "Cavalry" and "other arms"—a distinction which is generally irrelevant, since all Arms are linked together by that great common denominator, the firearm. I have already noted how the presence of artillery dissipates "purely Cavalry tactical principles." Modern artillery fire, he says, necessitates deployment at 6,500 yards from the enemy at least. That is nearly four miles away, and the questions at once arise, Who are these invisible troops with Artillery? What is their strength and composition? Have they some of those troublesome cyclists and Infantry, or some of those unorthodox Mounted Infantry or Cavalry acting improperly as Mounted Infantry, who will make an additional complication in a situation already compromised by Artillery?

The German Regulations are superbly indifferent to these questions, and accordingly come in for fresh condemnation. Cavalry are supposed to know at four miles what the composition, strength, and intentions of the enemy are, and if the enemy is Cavalry (the cyclists and Infantry prescribed by the Regulations themselves are ignored), the echelon system (previously outlined) is to provide for all contingencies. The author pitilessly dissects this childlike scheme. "In peace manœuvres," he remarks caustically, "there is always a tacit understanding that the enemy is no stronger than one's own force." In war it is otherwise. To clear up the situation "energetic contact with the enemy by fire-action is necessary." "Only by a protracted action can the enemy be forced to disclose his strength and intentions," and "a protracted fight can only be carried out by fire-action." Perfectly sound, we agree; and then we remember, with a start, those terrible led horses, and the doctrines founded on them. "It is only when conscious of a great moral and tactical superiority, or when there is any prospect of surprising the enemy, that an attack should be dared without the necessary numerical preponderance." In other words, the author once more categorically contradicts himself. After first saying that fire-action—and "protracted," "energetic" fire-action—is the only means of forcing the enemy to disclose his strength and intentions, he adds in the next breath that such action is on no account to be undertaken unless the enemy's strength is already known, and he is known to be greatly inferior, either numerically, or tactically and morally! Is it any matter of surprise that the Germans are slow to listen to General von Bernhardi?

The same deadly instinct for self-refutation dogs the General through his satire on the regulation method of "passing a defile" (p. 154). In peace "one side is kept as far from the defile as possible, in order that the passage on the other side may be possible," and that both may have the luxury of a knightly combat. These practices the General prophesies will lead to "enormous losses in war," and he pleads for a modicum of commonplace fire-action. "Whether," he gravely remarks, "the attack be undertaken mounted or dismounted will depend upon the attitude of the enemy and the attendant circumstances." Yes, but we know from other sources what that means—namely, that if the enemy shows a "defensive attitude," the attack will be by fire; but that there will be no attack at all, even so, unless he is greatly inferior, either morally and tactically or numerically.

Later we have a condemnation of Regulation No. 519, which directs the Army Cavalry, not only to drive the hostile Cavalry from the field, but to press back or break through "detachments of all arms." "I cannot conceive," says the General, "any real case in which Cavalry can break through hostile detachments of all arms." Poor Cavalry! If mounted riflemen laboured under such a disability, there would have been no South African War at all—literally none.

Then Regulation No. 403 falls a victim. It is certainly an easy prey. "Personal observation [*i.e.*, by the commander] is always the best, and is *essential in the case of offensive action against Cavalry*." The Regulations, of course, assume that both Cavalries disdain to use their rifles, and whirl about in huge ordered masses up to the moment of contact; but the author plaintively argues that fire rules the situation, and makes the zone of combat such that it is utterly impossible for one individual to have ocular perception of all that is going on. "One brigade will often fight on foot, the other mounted," he complains, "so that a handling of a division according to rule is practically impossible." True comment, but how futile!

Then, conscious (as he so often is conscious) that his counsels may have a damping effect on his hearers, he ends in a burst of poetry. "The enemy's fire must not paralyze the idea of offensive action" (he means shock, though he does not like to say so). "We must act 'regardless of consequences,' 'wrest victory,'" etc., according to the hackneyed Cavalry phraseology, upon which modern war throws such a pitilessly searching light.

The next section, "Attack of Localities," needs little further comment. This attack must be done exclusively by fire, but in practice it can never be done. That is the only deduction we can arrive at. But there is one highly important point. At the end of the section the bewildered reader finds himself involved in a lengthy discussion on the sword and lance in mounted combat—a discussion from which I have already quoted, and which arises out of a radically false analogy between those steel weapons and the bayonet carried by the foot-soldier. If Cavalry have to do the same work as Infantry, should not they carry bayonets? That is how the debate arises. It is an interesting debate, on which anyone must frankly admit there may be legitimate difference of opinion. Even for Infantry the bayonet is somewhat under a cloud, as the General himself contends; and Mounted Infantry, or Cavalry acting as such, have powers of surprise and envelopment derived from the horse which may perhaps be held to compensate them for the doubtful advantage of a bayonet. Instead of reasoning thus, the General treats the bayonet only as a possible *substitute* for the sword, and rejects it on that ground. But what has the sword to do with the bayonet? The sword is meant for use on horseback; the bayonet is fixed to the rifle, and is used on foot as a factor in fire-tactics. The essence of the whole controversy we are engaged upon is whether it is any longer possible in modern war to fight on *horseback*, and whether the rifle should not be the weapon *par excellence* of mounted troops. Whether you reinforce it with the bayonet or not is a distinct question, which has no relation whatever to the value of the sword and lance. It seems absolutely hopeless to get this distinction grasped. Over and over again in the letters and articles on this controversy the same old fallacy recurs, and, as I shall show later, it influences the German General more deeply than he realizes.

The section on "Defence" (p. 176) is short, and mainly consists of the elaborated truism that all defence should have an offensive character. The General seems to think that this maxim applies especially to Cavalry. It is the old delusion that Cavalry is a more offensive Arm than Infantry, and it leads him inexorably to the fatal conclusion that Cavalry cannot be trusted to undertake a "completely passive defence." They will only attempt to do so—but observe the comprehensive breadth of the exceptions—when it is a case of "holding a crossing over some obstacle, defending an isolated locality, or gaining time." In these cases a retirement may be involved "which is difficult to carry out on account of the led horses, and *should only be attempted in very favourable country*. It demands that the fight shall be broken off—always a difficult matter, and, to Cavalry *encumbered* by these led horses, one of considerable danger." "Remounting when pressed by the enemy is always a critical matter." It makes one hot to hear this sort of thing commended to British soldiers by Sir John French. It spells disgrace in war. Troops who cannot break off a fight cannot fight at all. "Colonel X., be good enough to cover my retreat with your regiment. Defend that crossing, please, or that locality, and gain me time." "Very sorry, sir, but the ground is unfavourable, and my led horses encumber me." Supposing our gallant Colonials had said that at Sannah's Post? They found, indeed, how "critical a matter" it is to remount when pressed by the enemy, for the Boers charged right into them again and again; but they did not flinch, and they saved their column from ruin, while the Cavalry engaged, equally brave men, but ignorant of their true rôle in war, failed in the task set them. But all this is "abnormal," Sir John French would say. A respectable hostile Cavalry would have summoned us to knightly combats with the steel.

And then (on p. 184) we come, as usual, to the corresponding *reductio ad absurdum*. "In mounted combat [*i.e.*, with the steel] the breaking off of the fight is quite impossible. Troops once engaged must carry the fight through. Even when retreating from the mêlée fighting Cavalry has no means of extricating itself. It is then entirely dependent on the enemy, and can only retire at the most rapid speed," etc. "Whoever expects to rally a beaten Cavalry division after a mounted fight by blowing the divisional call lays himself open to bitter disappointment."

No wonder so much stress is laid on the offensive character

of Cavalry!

We have now completed our review of the author's theories on the action of the Independent Cavalry, and I must ask the reader for a moment to compare with his views the instruction on the same topics contained in our own Manual, "Cavalry Training." The same fundamental error vitiates the whole of this instruction, but in an infinitely more mischievous form. The German author makes both shock and fire equally absurd, but his respect for shock never deters him from telling in his own strange way home-truths about fire which at least force the reader to construct for himself cosmos out of chaos. Our authorities, conscious that the intermingling of shock and fire will create difficulties only too apparent to Englishmen with any knowledge or memory of South Africa, divorce them completely from one another. In their Manual, Cavalry *acting against Cavalry*, whatever the terrain or other circumstances, are assumed never to employ fire-action, whose results are described as "negative," but only to employ shock. If the reader will turn to pages 196-212, which deal with the Independent or strategical Cavalry, he will observe with what really remarkable ingenuity the compilers manage to avoid even the remotest recognition of the fact that Cavalrymen carry rifles. The word "fire" is not breathed, though to the intelligence even of the most ignorant layman it must be plain that fire must dominate and condition the functions described, especially those beginning with the "approach march when within striking distance of the hostile Cavalry" (p. 202).

The various problems bravely but confusedly tackled by General von Bernhardi are here quietly ignored. Everything is so arranged as to lead up without hitch to the physical collision on horseback of the two opposing Cavalry "masses." There is no echo of von Bernhardi's rule about early deployment in view of Artillery fire. Our own Artillery, it is true, is to "throw into confusion" the enemy's Cavalry—a compliment which no doubt the enemy may return (p. 208). But, confusion or no confusion, the climax is to be the purest of pure Cavalry fights. Scouts and patrols are to observe the enemy and to prevent our own commander from "engaging his brigades on unfavourable ground" (note that pregnant warning); but there is no suspicion or suggestion of von Bernhardi's "protracted fire-fight" in order to discover the strength and intentions of the enemy, especially in view of the possibility that the enemy may, with unsportsmanlike perversity, choose ground which is "unfavourable to our brigades." Our Cavalry Commander (p. 205), it is to be inferred, is to perform the physical impossibility enjoined by the German Regulations, and criticized by von Bernhardi (pp. 160-162), of personally overlooking the whole of the attack and the ground which it is to cover. Needless to say, there is not a whisper about those sinister prophecies of the German author that "one brigade will often fight on foot, the other mounted"; that it will be impossible "to put a division into the fight (*i.e.*, shock-fight) in proper cohesion"; that, in view of fire, "the situation during the rapidly changing phases of the Cavalry fight will often be quite different from what was expected when the tasks were allotted"; and that, fire apart, European topography is such that opportunities for the "collisions" of Cavalry masses will be very rare.

With our authorities all goes by clockwork on Frederician and Napoleonic lines. "The enemy should be surprised," so that the charge may follow immediately after the deployment. The attack is to be on the echelon system ridiculed by von Bernhardi, but the encounter, nevertheless, is not to be "broken up," but is to be by the "simultaneous

93

action of all brigades." The artless enemy co-operates, allows himself to be surprised upon the right piece of "favourable" ground, and courteously presents an objective which may be struck simultaneously. The Artillery of both sides ceases fire, fascinated by the sublime spectacle of the "collision"; the machine-guns, which have been "affording a means of developing fire *without dismounting*," also retire from business, and the knightly combat rages on its appointed level arena. Then comes the pursuit (p. 211). Troops are either to "pursue at top speed in disorder," or to "rally at once at the halt"; and on page 128 elaborate directions will be found for the practice of this "rally," which von Bernhardi says is an "absolute impossibility in war," and that it is "indeed astounding that we should give way to such self-deception." Is the rally, we wonder, one of the "best foreign customs" which Sir John French urges us to assimilate, or one of the worst, which he has accidentally overlooked?

It is only when our authorities have finished with the pursuit, which is to "completely exhaust and disorganize the beaten enemy," and when, the hostile Cavalrymen vanquished, our own Cavalry has been safely launched on its reconnoitring duties (p. 212), that they consider, under quite a distinct heading, and without a hint that it may have anything to do with what precedes, the dismounted action of Cavalry against what is described with judicious vagueness as an "enemy" (pp. 213-216). Then we have the same demoralizing injunction that von Bernhardi, in his fire-mood, so strongly combats—namely, that a "fire-fight is not to be protracted"; and the same equally vicious suggestion that von Bernhardi, in his steel-mood, acquiesces in—namely, that defence in any shape is a somewhat abnormal function of Cavalry; that they are not supposed to conduct stubborn defences ("tenacious" is Sir John French's own term); and that they should never demean themselves by constructing anything serious in the way of entrenchment (p. 215). But it is scarcely necessary to add that the led horses are not the nightmare to our authorities that they are to von Bernhardi, and that we do not yet stultify our own directions for fire-action by warnings about the minimum size of units, and the imperative need for moral, numerical, and tactical superiority. Yet these warnings are regarded, according to his own account, as inspired wisdom by Sir John French, whose own introductory remarks are conceived in an even more reactionary spirit than those of the "acknowledged authority" whom he recommends to British readers.

The finishing touches to the comedy of the shock-duel are given in the revised Mounted Infantry Manual of 1909; for, although in this connection the Cavalry Manual never breathes a word about its sister Arm, it is, as I have before mentioned, one of the regular duties of the Mounted Infantry to co-operate with the Cavalry, not only in reconnaissance, but in battle. Under the heading "Co-operation with Cavalry when Acting Offensively against Hostile Cavalry," the Mounted Infantry are to "seize points of tactical importance from which effective rifle and machine-gun fire can be brought to bear on the flanks of the opposing Cavalry before the moment of contact." We picture an amphitheatre, like Olympia, both rims of the horseshoe lined with hidden riflemen, and two solid blocks of Cavalry galloping towards one another in the arena below, and we are alarmed for the fate of the horsemen, exposed in such a formation to a sleet of bullets. But we come to a fortunate reservation. "Fire will rarely be opened upon the hostile Cavalry or Artillery until contact is imminent. The object aimed at is the defeat of the hostile Cavalry, and a premature opening of fire is liable to cause it to draw off and manœuvre, in order to bring off the Cavalry encounter outside effective rifle-range." Surely some humorist of the Mounted Infantry, coerced by the General Staff into finding a rôle for his Arm which should not trench upon the sacred preserves of the Cavalry, penned these exquisite lines by way of stealthy revenge! What delicate consideration for the "knightly" weapons! What an eye for theatrical effect! What precautions against the disturbance of the collision by the premature discharge of vulgar firearms! And what a tactful show of apprehension lest these reminders of the degenerate twentieth century should scare away the old-world pageant to regions beyond "effective rifle-range"! It will be noticed that even the Artillery of the enemy is to be immune until "contact is imminent"—a somewhat doubtful risk to take without a written guarantee from the enemy that his Artillery will reciprocate the courtesy. (For the Gunners' view, see below, p. 204.)

Finally, with what unerring neatness, under his veil of genial irony, does our humorist manage to expose and satirize the futility of the lance and sword and the deadly pre-eminence of the rifle! He recognizes that it is only by the indulgence and self-restraint of riflemen that swords and lances can be used, and he knows, as we all know, that it is physically impossible for modern Cavalry, in war or peace, to find any spot on the globe which is "outside effective rifle-range"—unless they take the unsoldierly course of throwing away their own rifles. In peace, of course, as von Bernhardi constantly reminds us, rifles may be, and frequently are, ignored, even if they are not left in barracks; but in "real war" there is no use for troops who can only fight outside effective rifle-range. I need only add that the ideal Cavalry combat, as envisaged by our authorities, is precisely the combat which von Bernhardi stigmatizes in peace manœuvres as a "spectacular battle-piece." Mounted Infantry to him represent a force which, by "seizing the rifle," will "compel" the opposing Cavalry to "advance dismounted." The case imagined is what he regards as the normal case of "co-operation with other arms," and it will be remembered that "he can conceive no case in which Cavalry [*i.e.,* using the steel] can break through a hostile detachment of all arms."

One stands in awe before the almost miraculous tenacity of a belief which can give birth to such puerilities as I have quoted from our Manuals without perishing instantly under the ridicule of persons conversant with war. If the thing described had ever once happened, it would be different, but it never has happened, and never can or will happen. In war no Commander-in-Chief would tolerate even a tendency towards such child's-play. Otherwise, in pessimistic moments, one might tremble for the Navy. Supposing our Dreadnoughts were trained to withhold their fire so as to decoy hostile wooden three-deckers into collisions with our wooden three-deckers, and encounters settled by cutlasses on the lines of Salamis and Syracuse?

The parallel is not discourteous to the Cavalry. When they will it, they can be Dreadnoughts. But their shock-charge is as obsolete as sails and wood in naval war.

FOOTNOTES:

[4] "With them [the Cavalry] it will never be a case of prepared positions—which Cavalry as a rule will neither attack nor defend—but of actions resulting from a battle of encounter."

This is directly contradicted on p. 342, where it is laid down that "attacks on an enemy in position," as explicitly distinguished from "battles of encounter," are said to be "very necessary in time of war," and should be "repeatedly practised" in peace. The same injunction is repeated on pp. 343 and 345.

This is a typical example of the textual self-contradictions in which the book abounds.

CHAPTER VII

THE BATTLE OF ALL ARMS

I.—German Views.

WE have now come to the exposition of the part Cavalry will play in the great battle of all Arms, which, says von Bernhardi, is always "pre-arranged." But it will occur to the reader at once that, so far as our inquiry about fire and the steel in combat is concerned, there can be nothing new to be said. There are firearms in all warfare, and the tactical principles they enforce will be approximately constant. Every great battle takes the form of a series of "attacks on localities," or "battles of encounter," however we interpret those phrases. If an enemy, to whatever Arm belonging, who takes up a "defensive attitude" can only be attacked by fire in a fight of the Independent Cavalry, he can only be attacked by fire in a pre-arranged battle; and if the led horses are a paralyzing encumbrance in the one case, they are equally so in the other. The great battle, it is true, presents a more positive and obvious example of the co-operation of the various Arms; but, as we have seen, the co-operation "of other arms" has been regarded by the author as a normal incident of the combats he has already described, and the "purely Cavalry fight" as an altogether exceptional incident. And since even the purest Cavalry carry the rifle, they can at any moment sully the purity of the said fight by resort to that sordid but formidable weapon.

The author, as we might expect, only dimly appreciates the universality of his own principles—if the mutually destructive propositions which he alternately lays down can be properly termed principles. He constantly confuses tactics with combat. Different rules, of course, must always govern the action of mounted troops and horseless troops, because the one class is more mobile than the other; but it is impossible to lay down any lucid and intelligible principles for modern war until we realize the ubiquity and the supremacy of the missile weapon, rifle or gun.

The Army Cavalry, he tells us, as distinct from the divisional Cavalry, "must be engaged *en masse,* and not in detail." "It must simultaneously engage its whole fighting strength," as an undivided entity (p. 190 *et seq.*), and its proper position is forward of one of the flanks. We have no sooner grasped this principle than we find a separate chapter devoted to the action of "those portions of the Cavalry which find themselves behind the fighting-line, not on the exposed flank." This subdivision, we are vaguely told, "may be the result of circumstances," but there is no indication of what those circumstances are. But this is only one infraction of the principle of unity. In spite of the distractingly vague use of terms such as "front" and "flank," "enemy," "hostile forces," "troops within hostile reach," we are able to distinguish the following functions for the Cavalry mass during the battle:

It must conduct (1) a "far-reaching exploration" on the enemy's extreme rear and "probable lines of approach and communication," so as to give warning of the approach of fresh reserves; (2) an "immediate tactical reconnaissance," evidently of the whole battle-front—though the vague expression "against such hostile troops as may be within tactical reach" might mean almost anything. But we are told explicitly later that during the whole course of the battle the Cavalry mass "must in all cases prevent the enemy's patrols from making observations as to the disposition of our own *Army*, while, on the other hand, its own reconnaissance should never cease" (p. 199). We receive a sort of mental dislocation, therefore, when the author resumes: "Screened by these various measures, the Cavalry mass now advances fully deployed for the fight." Were "these measures," then, only to screen the Cavalry mass? But how can detachments, perhaps twenty miles away on the other flank, be said to screen the Cavalry mass? (3) The mass is to provide for the occupation of "defiles and other important places to the flank and front of the main body" (*i.e.*, of the main *Army*).

Let us pause and think. Supposing the initial battle-front is thirty or forty miles in extent. Even in the Boer War it was frequently thirty miles, while in Manchuria the fronts were sometimes enormously more extensive—at Mukden nearly 100 miles. How in the world is the entire Cavalry mass, *posted outside one flank*, to provide for the continuous reconnaissance, close and distant, of such a front, the occupation of advanced points, and for the maintenance of a reserve behind the front, while remaining a practically undivided force for united action? What is the enemy's Cavalry supposed to be doing? In theory, we are told, they will do the right thing, that is, post themselves by instinct outside one flank exactly opposite our own mass. But supposing they do not. Whatever they do, they have got (4) to be "driven from the field" (the reader will recollect the well-known formula), which will involve dispersion, if they disperse. But the author is not nearly so strong on the formula as Sir John French. It is a very small matter (p. 191), this driving of the hostile Cavalry from the field. "It has a certain value, but is comparatively useless for the main issue of the battle, unless, further, the possibility is gained of intervening in the decisive battle of all arms."

Is not the reader conscious of an extraordinary artificiality and unreality in the terms employed? Why speak of Cavalry driving the hostile Cavalry off the field, with more emphasis than of Infantry doing the same to Infantry? Presumably, because Cavalry, as we have already learnt, cannot break off the fight either in their pure or debased capacity. But on page 198 the beaten Cavalry is to "seek shelter behind occupied points of support," where it is to be attacked by the greatest possible fire-power, words which seem to imply that hitherto the attack has been by shock. Yet we have had it laid down as an axiom that neither party to a shock-combat can be used as a manageable unit for an indefinite time.

(5) The indivisible mass is now subject to fresh disintegration. "All portions of it not required for the pursuit" just described are to "regain their tactical cohesion" (an admission that the whole has lost its tactical cohesion), and, leaving their comrades to carry on the fire-fight, which may, of course, last for a week or more, are "to prepare for fresh effort." They are to occupy "localities" near the ground won, and "garrison" them with dismounted men — a direction we can scarcely take seriously when we recollect the crushing disabilities under which Cavalry acting in passive defence have been supposed by the author to labour (see *supra*, pp. 122-123).

(6) What is left of the mass now "takes up a position of readiness" secure from the view and fire of the enemy, and

disposed in what the author calls "groups of units." The expression seems to lack precision, but "this is the most suitable formation." Subsequent action is to be according to the "circumstances of the various cases," and it is here that the reminder is casually interpolated that a protective and offensive reconnaissance along the whole battle-line is to be a continuous duty of the mass. But this action is "not to be regarded as sufficient." "The mass is to insure its own advance to that portion of the field where the decisive battle will probably take place, so that the charge will not meet with unexpected resistance and obstacles when the moment comes to ride it home. When this crisis of the battle approaches, the Cavalry must be ready to intervene.... As the crisis approaches, endeavours must be made to get as close to the enemy as possible, in order to shorten the distance that will have to be covered in the charge." Observe how naturally, how mechanically, the author associates the "crisis" with a gigantic Cavalry charge, and with what simple trustfulness he believes that unexpected resistance and obstacles will melt away, if only the mass can insure its advance to the right spot in time.

As I shall show, he ruthlessly shatters his own hypothesis in the next breath; but consider, in the light of "real war," the utter futility of all this so-called instruction for the "pre-arranged battle," with its pre-arranged crisis. Note the complete neglect of all the really important factors, the tremendous power of modern rifles and guns, and the vast extent and duration of modern battles, as contrasted with the limited physical powers of the horse and the small proportion which Cavalry in all armies bears to other Arms. Take Liao-yang, the Sha-Ho, Mukden, battles which lasted ten days, two weeks, and three weeks, and try and find from the author's remarks any practical, tangible guidance for such situations. Fancy one indivisible mass maintaining a continuous reconnaissance over such distances, occupying defiles and "localities" to the front, leaving a reserve behind the battle-front, driving the entire hostile Cavalry from the field, and utterly destroying its power of further action; garrisoning points in the ground won, and at the same time advancing towards the "probable" point of crisis. But this point may be two days' march from the flank, where the mass—or what remains of it—was posted, and when it gets there it will certainly find that the crisis is centring round some strong, defensible position where lances and swords will be less useful than bows and arrows. No such picture as the author draws occurred in the Franco-German, Austro-Prussian, or Russo-Turkish Wars. It did not occur at Vionville, the only battle in which a situation came about even approximately resembling the circumstances he outlines. So far as there was a crisis there, and so far as it was dealt with by a Cavalry charge, the circumstances have radically altered, and there is a "total absence of analogy," as the author himself expressly states. Bredow's steel-charge was made against unbroken Infantry and Artillery, flushed with the hope of victory. Such charges, he has told us with truth, are utterly impossible in modern war. "I cannot conceive any real case in which Cavalry can break through detachments of all arms" (p. 160). "Nowadays, when Infantry can cover the ground to a distance of 1,500 or even 2,000 yards with a hot and rapid fire, and offer in their wide extension no sort of objective for shock-action, an attack on unshaken, steadily-firing Infantry, which has any sort of adequate field of fire, is *quite out of the question*" (p. 127).

It seems odd to have to recall these matters, for the author, as I said before, shatters his own hypothesis in the paragraphs immediately following his pages on the crisis and the charge. "However important and desirable it may be to contribute to the great decision by a glorious Cavalry

103

charge, it should be borne in mind that the possibility of this will occur in very rare cases." He goes on to insist emphatically on this point, saying nothing here about the vastly enhanced effect of the modern rifle, but basing his argument on terrain. Great charges, he says, were almost impracticable in the Franco-Prussian, Russo-Turkish, and Manchurian Wars, and "possible European theatres of war are but little suitable for charges, owing to the extent to which they have been cultivated." Peace operations are of no practical significance, because uncultivated country is expressly chosen. And so on.

Then, why, we ask, all this reasoned instruction about Cavalry making its way to the crisis and delivering its charge? Why not have said at the outset that their normal action must be something quite different? Instruction for remote improbabilities is practically useless. What the commander wants to know is what to do as a general rule, especially when a wrong decision may, owing to the extent of the battle-field, involve him in ignominious impotence. Such is Cavalry literature. Serious men in any other walk of life would not tolerate exposition of this sort.

We discover now that the Cavalry are not, after all, to make their way to the crisis and charge. That was conventional rhetoric. In reality they are to *act on the rear of the hostile army,* "upon the reserves, the column of supply, the heavy Artillery, etc." "It is here that opportunities for decisive action must be sought." Well, obviously that is a different proposition altogether. Why not have begun with it? Habit —just the irresistible habit of associating Cavalry with shock, and of calling shock their "proper rôle," although it is only their "exceptional" rôle. For, of course, such action as the author now indicates is purely a matter of fire. That is why no such decisive attack upon the rear of a great Army has ever in recent times been accomplished by European

Cavalry. The Cavalries of the sixties and seventies in the last century were absolutely incapable of such action, owing to their lack of fire-power. He is no doubt thinking of his model war, the American struggle of 1861-1865, and if he were truly candid, he would tell his countrymen that the brilliant exploits of the Civil War leaders in raiding communications and "hostile reserves" were performed solely through the rifle.

The author is perfectly aware that the modern rifle has five times the power of the rifle of 1865, but he has not the courage of his own opinions, and descends to misty compromise. "Such action must, of course, be conducted with a due co-operation between mounted and dismounted action." What is the use of a rule like that? "Against intact hostile reserves the firearm will be principally used." Why "principally"? Will not these intact reserves, to say the least, "take up a defensive attitude," and therefore render a fire-attack, according to his own repeatedly formulated rule, absolutely indispensable? "Against columns of waggons it will be well to commence by fire-action." Why "commence" only? Is there no lesson from South Africa here? On what single occasion were lances and swords of the smallest value in attacks on transport? Not on one. And on how many occasions did mounted riflemen, destitute of these weapons, capture transport and guns and rout reserves? We all know —Sir John French knows—what our troops suffered in this way. Why does he not warn his countrymen, instead of telling them that these German speculations are brilliant, logical, conclusive, complete?

Look once more at the great Manchurian battles. Observe, for example, the great battle of Mukden, (with its awful record of massacre by firearms), when a Japanese Cavalry brigade, acting with Nogi's turning force, endeavoured to operate on the Russian rear. It was miserably weak numerically, and it failed to accomplish anything "decisive"; but it did wonders, as it was, purely through fire. Has any critic, however enamoured of the *arme blanche*, ever suggested that, however strong, it could have accomplished anything with the lance and sword? The very suggestion is preposterous. Fire ruled that terrific struggle from first to last. Look at Mishchenko's pitiful Cavalry raid on the Japanese communications in January, 1905; and observe the shame which overtakes Cavalry who cannot fight on foot: whole brigades paralyzed by squads of isolated riflemen, reminding us only too painfully of Dronfield and Poplar Grove; Cossacks pathetically charging stone walls with drawn swords; disaster and humiliation clouding the whole sordid drama. Sir John French's contribution to our enlightenment on the Manchurian War, in his Introduction to Bernhardi's first book, "Cavalry in Future Wars," was that the Cossacks failed through excess of training as riflemen. He has not repeated that statement in his Introduction to the second book. He scarcely could.

All the world knows the truth now—namely, that the Cossacks, as one who rode with them said, "once dismounted, were lost." They did not know how to handle rifles, and all their humiliations may be traced to that fact. Nor did the Japanese Cavalry at first, and they were equally impotent. But they learnt, and learnt to admirable purpose, as the records show. If he cannot repeat and confirm what he said in his first Introduction, why is Sir John French altogether silent on the point in his second Introduction? Well, it was an awkward dilemma for him; for Bernhardi himself (p. 97), in his chapter on Raids, alludes to Mishchenko's raid in highly significant, though characteristically obscure, language. And if he follows up the clue, the reader may understand why it is that only on this one solitary question of raids, out of all the multitude of topics dealt with in the two books, Sir John French "ventures to differ" from the German author, pronouncing, for his own part, against them. Von Bernhardi expressly founds his advocacy of the raid on the American Civil War. "The idea," he says naïvely, "is taken" from that war. As though the Boers who made the raids of 1901, of which he never seems to have heard, took their ideas from that war or any other! Their ideas were the fruit of their own common sense. Now, the Civil War is particularly dangerous ground in England for advocates of the *arme blanche*, although it is safe enough ground in Germany, where nobody studies it, and where there has been no Henderson to immortalize the exploits of the great Cavalry leaders. Fire, and fire alone, rendered the American raids possible.

I need scarcely say that there is no incongruity in discussing together the raid proper and the attack on the reserves and communications of a great Army from which my digression originated. The weapon factor is precisely the same in both. Rifles are rifles and lances are lances, whatever the strategical or tactical scheme which bring them into play.

We turn lastly to the rôle of that portion of theoretically indivisible Cavalry mass which is maintained as a "reserve behind the front" (p. 204). The author's method is the same: first, to expound at length the duties and powers of this body as though they were its normal duties and powers, and then to state that these normal duties and powers—in other words, the "proper rôle"—of the force concerned are, in nine cases out of ten, impracticable and visionary. He first represents the great mounted charge as the primary object, the great mounted charge, moreover, against *Infantry*; for in this case there will be little chance, he says, of having "to deal with the hostile Cavalry." He proceeds to lay down the truly delightful maxim that the force is to mass behind "that part of the fighting line where the ground is adapted for a charge of large masses," though he has taken great trouble to show in the previous chapter, quite correctly, that this is precisely the kind of ground upon which important struggles will not centre. Then, in flat defiance of all he has said about charges against Infantry, he advocates what in effect is our old discredited friend the "death ride" against unshaken and victorious Infantry (p. 208), "in order to relieve our own exhausted Infantry," etc. The Cavalry are to "ride through the hostile Infantry, and fall upon the Artillery," although we know already that the author "can conceive no case in which Cavalry can break through detachments of all arms," and that an enemy who takes up even a defensive attitude can only be attacked by dismounted action. But in a flash of recollection of a prior maxim, he enjoins that not only the preliminary deployment, but the formation for attack in widely extended order, must take place "beyond the effective range of the enemy's fire"; for "once outside this zone ... nothing else can be done but to gallop straight for the front." Beyond the effective range of the enemy's fire! What is that range? He has told us before that it must, for average purposes, be reckoned 6,500 yards, or nearly four miles. Conceive a charge of four miles, begun out of sight of the enemy, and in the blissful confidence that at the end of it the "ground will be suitable" for fighting on horseback with steel weapons! He proceeds in this strain for four pages, elaborating his topic with detailed tactical instructions, and then comes the usual nullifying paragraph:

"It must be clearly understood that in this case, as in the other where the Cavalry is on the flank of the army, there will seldom be an opportunity for a charge." What, then, if not a charge? Half a page of fervid generalization. "The first essential is that victory shall be won.... The Cavalry must not shrink from employing its whole force on the fire-fight."

We are bidden, rightly enough, to study the ancient lesson of Fredericksburg. But it is now 1911. And we know what the author's views of the fire-fight for Cavalry are—that, owing to the burden of led horses, it is never on any account to be attempted, unless there is an assurance of complete moral, tactical, and numerical superiority. *Cadit quæstio* once more. Our reserve becomes a dummy.

There remain two topics in connection with the great pre-arranged battle of all arms—"Pursuit and Retreat" and the "Rôle of the Divisional Cavalry." I shall take the latter first, and, with little comment, merely appeal to the reader's sense of humour. "In the battle of all arms," says the General, "as soon as fighting contact has been established with the enemy, and the close and combat reconnaissance is then probably at an end, the divisional Cavalry must endeavour to gain touch with the Army Cavalry in order to strengthen the latter for the battle. In so doing it must not, of course, lose all connection with its own Infantry division." Remember that the Army Cavalry is, by hypothesis, well outside our flank of a battle area which may be of any extent from ten to seventy miles. Picture the various divisional Cavalries along this front endeavouring to "gain touch" with the Army Cavalry, while not losing connection with their own respective divisions.

It may be that this particular injunction has aroused merriment in Germany. That is not our business. But that Sir John French, with undisturbed gravity, should solemnly pass it on to Englishmen as the last word of military wisdom—that is extraordinary. Observe that, as usual, the *arme blanche* is responsible for the aberrations of the German writer. In the succeeding sentence this becomes clear. "When this cannot be done, and *when no other chance of mounted action offers*, the divisional Cavalry must seize the rifle, and act as an immediate support for the Infantry." The words I have italicized show that the physical feats contemplated in the original injunction are to be performed in the interests of shock, and that, if in the cold prosaic light of day they daunt the imagination of the leaders on the field, there is nothing left but to "seize the rifle."

"Pursuit and Retreat" is a chapter which almost defies any brief analysis. Only those who are thoroughly acquainted with the curiously ambiguous vocabulary which hampers Cavalry writers at every turn can fully appreciate the bankruptcy of the steel weapons as disclosed in these pages, and, at the same time, the disastrous effect of these useless bits of steel upon the reasoning faculties of those who still believe in them. The first few pages leave us only the impression that both pursuit and retreat are very dubious topics for Cavalry. We approach the kernel of the matter at p. 215, where the writer deprecates "direct frontal pursuits," which "will generally yield but meagre results against the masses of the modern Army and the firearm of the present day." The enemy will occupy "localities, woods, and the like," and "bring the Cavalry pursuit to a standstill." "Only when completely demoralized troops are retreating in the open, and cannot be reached by fire" (what this last clause means I cannot conceive), "will a charge be feasible." Very good; but why not have followed the same principle in earlier chapters, instead of talking of Cavalry charging Infantry under cover, etc.? "Frontal pursuit is essentially a matter for the Infantry, who must press the retreating enemy to the utmost." This seems a fairly definite rule, but we have no sooner grasped it than it is cancelled.

"On the other hand, it is, of course, the duty of the Cavalry to maintain touch with the enemy under all circumstances. With this object in view, it must continue the *frontal pursuit*, sometimes even without seeking to draw on a fight, by day and night." How one can continue a *frontal* pursuit by day

110

and night without seeking to draw on a fight I leave the reader to guess. We turn to "Retreat," which is, of course, the counterpart of pursuit, only to be involved in a fresh tangle. Whether the enemy's Cavalry is assumed to be conducting a frontal pursuit by day and night in spite of its "meagre results," or whether our own Infantry are bearing the brunt of the retreat in the face of the frontal pursuit of the enemy's Infantry—a pursuit which is "essentially" their business—we are left in uncertainty. All we have are vague heroics about the "maintenance of morale" (the writer seems to be very nervous about the morale of Cavalry), about never renouncing a "relentless offensive," and about attacking the "enemy," wherever possible, with the cold steel. We find ourselves wondering how it is that "completely demoralized troops retreating in the open" (by hypothesis the only proper subjects for a steel-charge) can be, nevertheless, conducting a victorious pursuit, and our only escape from the entanglement is that in the case now considered by the author "enemy" means "Cavalry," who are, apparently, so far inferior to Infantry (though they carry the very weapon which makes Infantry formidable) that they can be "relentlessly attacked," even when they are not completely demoralized.

One soon ceases to be surprised at anything in this species of literature, or one would gasp with amazement at the levity with which Cavalrymen throw ridicule on their own Arm. Suddenly and very tardily we come upon an indication of the alternative to that frontal pursuit which gives such meagre results and yet must be continued day and night. "Thus, when it becomes no longer possible to show a front to the pursuing Cavalry in the open, measures must be taken to block the routes upon which his *parallel* pursuit is operating," etc. Does not the reader feel his brain going when he reads a sentence like this? What antithesis can there be between Cavalry "pursuing in the open" and Cavalry conducting a "parallel pursuit"? There is no more or less probability of open ground in a parallel than in a frontal pursuit. It is the old story. One half of the writer's brain is back in the days of Frederick the Great; the other half is in working in the medium of the present.

That is the key to this chapter, from which a Cavalry leader could not gain one concrete, definite rule for his guidance in real war. On pursuit, as on many other topics, the author was more clear and instructive in his earlier work, "Cavalry in Future Wars" (Chapter IV.), where he was not hampered by having to consider Regulations with any pretence to modernity, and where he accordingly spoke with freedom on the absolute necessity of fire-action in pursuit; though he could not even then wholly grasp the corollary, the absolute necessity of fire-action in retreat.

II. — THE BRITISH VIEW.

Let us now, as in the case of the fight of the Independent Cavalry, contrast the directions given by our own authorities for the great battle of all Arms ("Cavalry Training," pp. 225-229). One point of difference we may dispose of at once. The divisional Cavalry (who are Mounted Infantry) and the "protective" Cavalry (to which there is no German counterpart) behave rationally. They remain with, or drop back to, their respective main bodies, and there make themselves generally useful. The rules for the Independent or Army Cavalry, on the other hand, present a curious study. On the German model, this main mass is, generally speaking, to be posted forward of one of the flanks. (There is no suggestion of a "reserve behind the front.") But we notice at once, with some surprise, that nothing is said about the corresponding hostile Cavalry mass, which, according to von Bernhardi, should be the primary objective, and whose "absolute and complete overthrow" is, according to Sir John French (p. xiv), a "primary necessity."

The explanation is that one of the opposing Cavalry masses is assumed to have been already absolutely and completely overthrown—that is, during the pre-battle reconnaissance phase, whose central incident, as described in pp. 192-194 and 200-212 of the Manual, and criticized by me in the last chapter, is the great shock-duel of the two Independent Cavalries—a duel which is to result in the annihilation of one side or the other, and to which I shall have to return once more in the next chapter. The thread is resumed on p. 224 with the words, "Once the Independent Cavalry has defeated its opponent," etc., and from that point onwards nothing is heard of the hostile Independent Cavalry. The explanation of Sir John French's expression is the same. On p. xv he, too, assumes that *before the battle* the hostile Cavalry has been disposed of, and says, somewhat vaguely, that the "true rôle of Cavalry on the battle-field is to reconnoitre, to deceive, and finally to support"—functions which he distinctly suggests should be carried out mainly through fire-action by troops "accustomed to act in large bodies dismounted." And we seem to recognize this view in the functions outlined in the Manual on p. 225. "Reconnoitre," it is true, disappears. We find no echo of von Bernhardi's chimerical conception of a double reconnaissance, distant and close, along the whole battle-front; nor, we may add, of his injunction to "occupy defiles and other important places to the flanks and front" of the Army.

The rôles suggested for the flank Cavalry mass are:

1. To "act against the enemy's flanks."

2. To combine *fire* concentrically with the main attack.

3. To pursue on parallel lines—a function which it is laid

down on p. 229 is to be performed mainly with the rifle.

4. To force the enemy away from his direct line of retreat; which is merely a corollary of No. 3.

So far, good; but the *arme blanche*, as we might expect, is not going to be suppressed in this summary fashion, and when we pass from pious generalization to the actual "crisis," which "offers the greatest opportunities for Cavalry action," we breathe once more the intoxicating atmosphere of the great shock-charge, not against Cavalry now (for they are *ex hypothesi* extinct), but against Infantry and Artillery. There is a mild caution about the "modern bullet," but it is evidently not intended to be taken very seriously. The relation between the "flank" phase and functions and the "crisis" phase and functions is passed over in silence. Von Bernhardi's difficulty about deployment and advance under modern fire is surmounted by the simple direction that for what is called the "approach" surprise is essential; yet in the next breath "fire-swept zones" are envisaged which are to be passed over in a "series of rushes from shelter to shelter in the least vulnerable formation"—a process exclusive of surprise; and on the absolutely vital point of the formation for the actual attack one can positively watch the compilers struggling to reconcile Cromwellian principles with modern facts, and embodying the result in studiously vague and misleading language. The front of the Cavalry is not to be "too narrow," but the imperative necessity insisted on by von Bernhardi of *wide extension* in the whole attacking force is implicitly denied by the direction that "squadrons in extended order may be used to divert the enemy's attention from the *real attack*." Then, there is to be the stereotyped rally, which is to be in "mass," and the resulting mass is apparently to escape from further fire by using "another route."

When will our soldiers base their rules on war facts? As I

114

have said, the facts show that it is still possible, in certain conditions, for men on horses, big target as they are, to penetrate a modern fire-zone, and attack and defeat riflemen and Artillery; but it is impossible to do so if they insist on conforming their methods to the assumption that they are to do their killing work by remaining in the saddle and wielding steel weapons. That idea is fatal. It is that idea which promotes these rules about not too narrow fronts, these grotesque mounted rallies in mass, and this pregnant silence about the real point of interest—what actually happens when a line of horsemen, stirrup to stirrup, or in extended order, wielding lances and swords, impinges on an extended line of dismounted riflemen. We know from war experience that such a charge, stirrup to stirrup, is as extinct as the dodo, and is advocated in set terms by no rational being. It has not even been tried or contemplated since 1870. We know that the widely extended type has shared the fate of the other, because, with the loss of physical "shock," the steel weapons have lost their whole historical *raison d'être*. The only practicable mounted charge known to modern war is that of the mounted riflemen, who *fight up to the charge*, and use the only weapon which is effective against riflemen—namely, the rifle, fortified, if need be, by the bayonet. This charge is not an essential to victory. Heaven knows we lost guns and men and transport enough in South Africa without any mounted charging. The very object of a missile weapon is to overcome distance in a way that the lance and sword cannot overcome it. For all we know, even the mounted rifle charge may wholly disappear as science improves the firearm. But that improved firearm will itself rule combat, and banish into still remoter realms of memory the reign of the lance and sword.

I have excepted the case of the "utterly demoralized" enemy —utterly demoralized, of course, by *fire*. He is, naturally, fair game for any weapon, and experience proves that the firearm once more is incomparably the best weapon. Lances and swords are, relatively, slow, cumbrous, and ineffective. A magazine pistol used even from horseback is a better weapon than either.

Nothing is said by our authorities as to attack during the battle upon the enemy's reserves and transport, enterprises in which von Bernhardi, after dismissing as a rare exception the great shock-charge, concludes that Cavalry are to seek their decisive opportunities. We may assume that, like raids on communications, they are ruled out. But no alternative to the shock-charge at the crisis is suggested, for the parallel pursuit is, of course, a subsequent phase. There is only the ominous reservation that, if the *ground* is not favourable to the shock-charge, the "Cavalry commander must look for his chance elsewhere, *or wait for a more favourable opportunity*" (p. 227).

That is just what we have to fear. That was the old, narrow, ignorant outlook of the continental Cavalries, who were always waiting for favourable opportunities, and accounts for the idleness and lack of enterprise which von Moltke stigmatized in 1866, and for the paltry character of their performances as a whole, which von Bernhardi recognizes and condemns. It accounts for the miserable failure of the Cossacks in Manchuria, and explains the success of the Japanese Cavalry, once they realized the worthlessness of their German instruction and textbooks, and discovered for themselves the worth of the rifle as a stimulus to activity and mobility. Von Bernhardi says (p. 202): "The greatest imaginable error ... is to adopt a waiting attitude ... in order that the possibility of a great charge might not slip by unutilized." That error is precisely what we have to fear. Teach Cavalry that their lances and swords are their principal weapons, and that the rifle is a defensive weapon;

tell them that the "climax of training" is the steel charge, "since upon it depends the final result of the battle"; found their "spirit" on the steel; make it in theory their "proper rôle"; give it a vocabulary of stirring epithets, like "glorious," "relentless," "remorseless," and all the rest, and they are only too likely, eager for battle as they are, to "wait for favourable opportunities" which will never occur, when they ought to be busy and active with their horses and rifles.

The sections on pursuit and retreat are modelled on similar sections in von Bernhardi's earlier book, "Cavalry in Future Wars," and escape therefore some of the contradictions of the later work. Since they lay predominant stress on fire, we can only hope that their obvious blindness to the true reasons for fire does little harm. Pursuits, whether by Infantry or Cavalry, be they frontal, parallel, or intercepting, will always be governed by fire. The thing that really distinguishes Cavalry from Infantry is that they have horses, which give them a vast scope for a class of intercepting tactics which Infantry cannot undertake so easily. But even Infantry will be better at any form of pursuit than a purely shock-trained Cavalry. Sir John French would have intercepted the Boers, not only at Paardeberg, but at Poplar Grove, Karee Siding, Dewetsdorp, and Zand River, if his Cavalry had understood the rifle as well as they understood the horse. Retreat is the counterpart of pursuit, and the same principles apply. Cavalry ought to be able to fight a rearguard action better than Infantry, because, thanks to their mobility, they can choose defensive points more freely, hold them longer, and fall back to others quicker. But if they are taught that it is beneath them to entrench and to defend a fire-position with stubborn tenacity, and that their proper rôle is to be performing Frederician fantasias with the lance and sword, then they are likely, "in real war," to be relegated to a sphere "outside effective rifle-range," and to find their place usurped

117

by Infantry and mounted riflemen. There is very little to be known about rearguard actions which the Boers have not taught us, and yet they were, in Cavalry parlance, "defenceless"—in other words, steelless riflemen.

CHAPTER VIII

RECONNAISSANCE

I.—WEAPONS.

I COME lastly to the author's chapters on "Reconnaissance, Screening, and Raids." As I explained before, it is the critic's simplest course to leave them to the last, because, although they come first, they almost ignore the subject of weapons and combats, on the assumption, apparently, that the opposing Cavalries, at any rate in the first two of the functions in question, will, as a matter of course, fight with the lance and sword in the pure and proper fashion. But we have now considered and tested the worth of the author's views on combat and weapons, and can apply our criticisms to these chapters.

Combat and weapons are not wholly overlooked. At the very outset comes the maxim which I quoted further back, to the effect that "the essence of Cavalry lies in the offensive," and that for defence they are to "abandon their proper rôle and seize the rifle on foot." The reader can appreciate now the value of this maxim, when we are dealing, as the author in these chapters is dealing, with two opposing Cavalries who are assumed to be acting against one another independently of other Arms. To tell both these Cavalries that their essence lies in the offensive is, to say the least, a superfluous platitude. To say that it is only in defence that they are to "seize the rifle" is to say something wholly meaningless. Unless by seizing it they can force their antagonists also to relinquish shock as useless and to seize the rifle, they might as well not seize it at all. If they can force their antagonists to seize it—and the whole mass of modern experience shows that they can and do—then their antagonists, whether we call their rôle proper or improper, are acting in *offence* with the firearm, and the maxim is stultified—as, indeed, any maxim which applies medieval language to modern problems must be stultified. Experience shows that if you arm men with long-range, smokeless, accurate missile weapons, whatever their traditions of etiquette and sportsmanship in peace, they will in war use those weapons to the exclusion of lances, swords, battle-axes, scimitars, and the various other weapons which were highly formidable before the days of gunpowder, but which have steadily declined since the invention and the progressive improvement of arms of precision.

Besides this general maxim upon the functions of the rifle and the steel, there are a few incidental allusions which must be noticed. The reader will remember the rule as to the powerlessness of the squadron as a unit for fire-action. The rule is anticipated here in directions for reconnoitring squadrons (p. 44), which, even by night, are only to fight with the *arme blanche*, "because dismounted action is generally dangerous, and, on account of the weakness of the force, usually leads to failure"; and we wonder again how *both* of two opposing reconnoitring squadrons can "fail," and how such a situation is actually to be dealt with on such principles in "real war"—say in the hedge-bound country which covers two-thirds of England. We are also told (p. 57) that patrols, "on collision with the enemy's patrols," are to take action "in as offensive a spirit as possible, but after due reflection." "Should a charge promise any kind of success, the opponent must be attacked in the most determined way." Nothing is said about fire, but we are left with the impression that a fire-attack can be neither "offensive" nor "determined," and for the rest we have to be content with guidance like the following: "It does not promise success to attack the front of an advancing squadron under the apprehension that it is a single patrol."

One day's personal experience of modern war would teach the author the perilous futility of all these "speculative" conjectures. Has he forgotten altogether the power and purpose of the modern rifle—the rapidity, accuracy, and secrecy of its fire—when he speaks of patrols indulging in due reflection about their determined offensive charges? It is to be feared that at the hands of any but utterly incompetent troops his own contemplative patrols would receive short shrift. And the lesson of South Africa? It is hard to see why, in the matter of patrols at any rate, those three years of war should be regarded as abnormal. Yet it is the fact, as I must repeat, that no Cavalry patrol or scout from the beginning to the end of the war ever used the lance or sword; that in reconnaissance no Boer ever came near being hurt by those weapons; and, furthermore, that the Cavalry were consistently and thoroughly outmatched in reconnaissance, which was governed universally by the rifle. It was exactly the same in Manchuria. Instead of reminding his German *confrère* of these facts, Sir John French complains that the difficulty of the Cavalry in South Africa was that they had nothing to reconnoitre, while he implicitly approves and applauds the conception of the reflective charging patrol.

To clinch the matter, we need only remind ourselves that our own divisional mounted troops, whose sole weapon is the rifle, are entrusted not only with reconnaissance for their own division, but, in certain events, with exactly the same duties as the Independent and protective Cavalry. In these duties they will be pitted (in the event of a Continental war) against steel-armed Cavalry. If steel weapons were of any use, this would be criminal.

Such are the scanty clues as to combat which we obtain from the chapters on reconnaissance. It remains to ask, What is von Bernhardi's view upon the great question of the employment of the Army or Independent Cavalry (as distinguished from the divisional Cavalry) in the most important of all its functions in modern war—reconnaissance? I defy anyone to answer that question. So far as it is possible to construct any positive view from a series of obscure and contradictory propositions, it appears to be a view which is in direct conflict with that of Sir John French and of the Cavalry Manual which presumably he approves, while approving equally of General von Bernhardi. Anyone familiar with Cavalry literature will know of the old controversy between the theories of concentration and dispersion. Is the Army Cavalry at the opening of a campaign to concentrate and "drive from the field" the enemy's Army Cavalry, or is it from the outset to begin its work of exploring the various lines of approach of the various hostile columns over the whole front—an enormously extensive front—upon which great modern armies must develop their advance?

II.—THE PRELIMINARY SHOCK-DUEL.

In view of the great size and vast manœuvring areas of modern armies and of the small numbers and transcendently important reconnaissance duties of Cavalry, that question would, I think, be decided in favour of dispersion, were it not for the fatal influence of the *arme blanche*. But Cavalrymen must have the gigantic shock-duel which I described and criticized in Chapter IV., 2. The idea of dispersion for sporadic bickering and scouting before this imposing tournament has been arranged is unthinkable to them. Our Manual therefore (pp. 193, 194) sets forth in all its naked crudity the idea of the preliminary shock-duel between the *concentrated* masses of the two Independent (or strategical) Cavalries—a duel that cannot, it is expressly laid down, be conducted by fire-action, which is negative and inconclusive, but which, conducted with the steel, is assumed to result in the complete and final "overthrow" of one party or the other. One side, in the words of the Manual, is "disposed of," and the surviving party proceeds to disperse and reconnoitre undisturbed in the vast area of war.[5]

Needless to say, the theory is purely academic. Such things have never happened in any war, ancient or modern, and assuredly never will happen. One Cavalry or the other may be depended upon in the future to act at the last moment with common sense. If it does not at once set about its work of reconnaissance, it will, at any rate, shiver to pieces with fire the massed shock-formations of its opponent.

General von Bernhardi seems to be conscious of the weakness of the theory, though he cannot bring himself to shatter it outright. There are, of course, two distinct questions involved: (1) Should the Independent Cavalries concentrate at the outset? (2) If so, should the resulting collision be a shock-collision? Number 1 is at any rate open to debate. Number 2 is not, but it always confuses the discussion of Number 1. The General could dispose of Number 2 merely by references to other parts of his own work—to the passages, for example, where he says that not only in the great battles of all Arms, but in the contests of Independent Cavalries, shock-charges are only to be "rare" and "exceptional" events. For "squadrons, regiments, and even brigades, *unassisted by other arms*, the charge may often suffice for a decision. But where it is an affair of larger masses, it will never be possible to dispense with the co-operation of firearms" (p. 103). And there is the passage about modern European topography where he shows the physical difficulty of bringing about these combats. On the broader question (No. 1) he speaks with two voices. In direct contradiction of Sir John French's introductory remarks and of our own Manual, he says (p. 20) that the strategical Cavalry is not necessarily "to seek a tactical battle"; that it is "by no means its duty under all circumstances to seek out the enemy's Cavalry in order to defeat it," because "by such conduct it would allow the enemy's Cavalry to dictate its movements." "On the contrary, it must subordinate all else to the particular objects of reconnaissance," etc.

It is clearly in his mind that, since the various corps or columns which are the objects of reconnaissance may be "advancing to battle" on a total front of 50 to 100 miles (this is his own estimate, p. 81), it will be advisable to explore their zones of approach at once. But there are other passages which support the opposite principle: for example, on page 15: "The circumstances of modern war demand that great masses of mounted men shall be used as Army Cavalry and concentrated in the decisive direction.... The front of the army, therefore, can never be covered throughout its entire length by the Army Cavalry," etc. On page 87 also he is quite decisive in the same sense: "The universal principle most always good for Cavalry, that when a decisive struggle is in prospect all possible strength must be concentrated for it"— an unexceptional truism, applicable as it stands to all struggles, great or small, by land or sea, but in its context only too suggestive of the gigantic shock-duel.[6] But on the whole he stands committed to nothing more definite than the following: "It remains for the leader to make his preparations in full freedom, and to solve the task confided to him in his own way." Profoundly true, but not very helpful in an instructional treatise on war.

III.—DIVISIONAL RECONNAISSANCE.

The chapter on "Divisional Reconnaissance" is still less intelligible. It would be interesting to know how Sir John French would sum up its "logical" and "convincing" doctrines. The divisional Cavalry are in all cases to "cleave to the Infantry" (p. 75) of their respective divisions, yet they are to take the place of the Army Cavalry "when a concentration of that force in a decisive direction takes place" (another hint of the gigantic preliminary shock-duel), and are even to indulge in "strategical exploration" (pp. 72-75). In fact, these amazing super-Cavalry are to perform physical feats in reconnaissance analogous to the feats designed for them in the pre-arranged battle of all arms (*vide* p. 149). Yet they cannot "fight independently" even with the hostile divisional Cavalry, nor clear the way for their own patrols, nor find their own outposts (pp. 75-76).

And then we come to a passage which, quite parenthetically and as it were by accident, throws a searching light upon the many dark places of this volume. The divisional Cavalry, *inter alia*, is to perform the "close reconnaissance along by far the greater part of the front of the army." But the close reconnaissance, owing to the range of modern firearms, is "considerably more difficult." "It thus becomes possible for the Cavalryman in general to get no closer to the enemy than his rifle will carry" (p. 80). "*His* rifle," be it noted. And the hostile Cavalryman (surely an "enemy") is presumably in the same case. What, then, of the charging patrols and squadrons?

I suppose I should add that only two pages later (p. 82) the author, in a fit of remorse, rehabilitates the charging patrol. "Rude force can alone prevail, and recourse must be had to the sword." Rude force! The tragi-comic irony of it!

IV.—SCREENS.

As to the chapter on Screens, we can only respectfully appeal to Sir John French to explain it. The ordinary reader can only give up the problem of elucidation in despair. What is the connection with his previous chapters on reconnaissance? Is the "screen" something different from or supplementary to the normal reconnoitring, patrolling, and protective duties of the Army and divisional Cavalry, as described under the headings, "Main Body of the Army Cavalry," "Reconnoitring Squadrons," "Distant Patrols," "Divisional Reconnaissance," etc.? One would infer from the opening paragraph that it is something wholly different. "The idea of the screen," runs the opening sentence, "is first touched on in the 'Field Service Manual' of 1908; it is also, however, demanded by the conditions of modern war"; and from what follows we gather that the screen means an inner and purely *protective* cordon of Cavalry, as distinguished from a distant offensive reconnoitring cordon. The same distinction is drawn in page 13 of the first chapter of the book. This is the kind of distinction drawn by our own Manual, which, though it does not speak of a "screen," divides the Cavalry into three bodies—one "Independent" or "strategical," the second "protective," while the third is the divisional Cavalry. Logically, of course, the distinction has but a limited value, unless, indeed, one regards the protective force as merely a chain of stationary outposts or sentries. All reconnaissance must obviously be defensive as well as offensive, because it represents a conflict between two opposing parties. If the protective Cavalry are pressed, it is their duty, as the Manual does, in fact, lay down, not only to resist the scouts and patrols of the hostile force, but to find out the strength and disposition of that force, and even in certain cases, explicitly provided for, to take the place of the Independent Cavalry; just as it is the duty of the Independent Cavalry, not only to pierce the hostile Independent Cavalry and inform themselves of the strength and disposition of the hostile Army, but to resist similar action on the part of their opponents. These principles would be taken for granted, with a vast improvement in the simplicity of regulations, if it were not for the influence of the *arme blanche*, impelling Cavalry writers to call their Arm a peculiarly *offensive* Arm, and inspiring the grotesque idea of the great preliminary shock-duel for the opposing Independent Cavalries, who are both presumed to be perpetually in offence as regards one another.

Still, within reasonable and well-understood limits, the metaphorical term "screen," as denoting the protective aspect of a widespread observing force, is both useful and illuminating. To regard it, as General von Bernhardi does, as a brand-new idea, the result of "reflection and experience" on the needs of modern war, is to convict himself of ignorance of war. Screens of a sort there always have been and always must be: the only new factor is the vastly increased efficacy of modern firearms; and if he could bring himself to concentrate on that new factor, of whose importance he shows himself in other passages to be perfectly aware, he would be able to convert into an intelligible, practical scheme his strange medley of inconsequent generalizations. He is, of course, handicapped by the official Regulations, which, unlike our own, do not formally provide for a "protective Cavalry" as distinguished from the divisional Cavalry, and which seem to be more than usually obscure and confused in their theories about "offensive" and "defensive" screens, and in their hazy suggestions as to what troops are to perform the respective functions; but he cannot or will not see the fundamental fallacy which, like Puck in the play, is tricking and distracting the minds of those who framed the Regulations, and so he himself makes confusion worse confounded. The protective aspect of the screen is no sooner insisted on than it is forgotten, and we have a disquisition on the offensive screen, which appears to be only another name for the normal activities of the Army Cavalry, behind the "veil" formed by whom a second screen is to be established by the divisional Cavalry (p. 87).

This, however, is disconcerting, because in the previous chapter (p. 74) we have been told with emphasis that the Army Cavalry "in the most usual case" will not be able to reconnoitre the whole Army front, but will be "concentrated in a decisive direction," and that the divisional Cavalry in such cases, in spite of their unfitness for the task, will have to do the "distant reconnaissance" and "strategical exploration" at all points not directly covered by the main Cavalry mass. And, sure enough, the "veil" just alluded to now disappears in its character as veil, and reappears as a "concentrated" mass. "The principal task of the offensive screen is to defeat the hostile Cavalry, and for this object all available force must be concentrated, for one cannot be strong upon the field of battle" (p. 87). It is amazing that serious exponents of any *métier* should write in this fashion. A concentrated screen is a contradiction in terms.

Once committed, however, the General persists. All cyclist detachments and patrols are "to be brought up to the fight" from everywhere. Roads are not to be blocked (in accordance with the screen idea) until the supreme Cavalry struggle, with its conventional "complete overthrow" of the hostile Cavalry, is over; and all this in flat contradiction of at least two-thirds of the earlier chapter on the Army Cavalry, where it was laid down that reconnoitring squadrons were from the first to be pushed forward from the "various groups of Army Cavalry," and were to be allotted reconnaissance zones; that a separation of Cavalry force was far the most probable line of action; and that reconnaissance was "an every-day task of the Cavalry," its "daily bread," a "duty which should never cease to be performed" for a single moment.

And yet on page 89 we come to the staggering, if cryptic, conclusion that "the Army Cavalry will only undertake an offensive screen when the Army is advancing and where the country does not afford suitable localities for the establishment of a defensive screen."

The writer then enlarges on the merits of the defensive screen, and, now that his mind is occupied with the idea of defence, makes it perfectly clear that the rifle is absolute master of the situation for the patrols, troops, squadrons, or any other units of both belligerent parties. Your defensive screen acts by fire, and obviously, therefore, whoever tries to pierce your screen must act by fire. These pages reduce to nullity all the romantic hints elsewhere about the charging patrol or squadron, with its "rude force" and its "determined" and "remorseless" attacks.

And what of illustrations and examples from modern war? Not one. Nothing but "speculative and theoretical reflection." For anyone who cares to study them, the facts are there—plain, hard, incontrovertible, convincing facts. Sir John French knows all about the South African facts. Screens, on a small or great scale, were matters of daily experience. He himself, with a force of all arms, sustained a screen for two months—primarily protective, but tactically offensive, as all screens must be—in the Colesberg operations of November-January, 1899-1900. He knows perfectly well that lances and swords, for all the use made of them, might as well have been in store, and that the Cavalry engaged acted on precisely the same principles as the Colonial mounted riflemen engaged.

During most of the operations from Bloemfontein to Pretoria, and from Pretoria to Komati Poort, our great force of all arms was pitted against what (if we consider relative numbers) was little more than a mounted screen, and every day's operations exemplified the fighting principles involved. The rifle was the great ruling factor. If the rifleman had a horse, so much the better—he was a more mobile rifleman; but lances and swords were useless dead-weight. Precisely the same phenomena reappear in Manchuria. On the Japanese side much excellent screening work was done by Infantry, against whom the Cossack scouts and reconnoitring squadrons, trained solely to shock, were impotent. Infantry move slowly, but their rifle is a good rifle, and it is not the horse which fires it, but the man. No infantry patrol of any Army—certainly, at any rate, of our own Army—is afraid of the lances or swords of a Cavalry patrol. It is only—strange paradox!—Cavalry patrols who are taught to fear the lances and swords of other Cavalry patrols.

I am reminded here of some remarks made in a letter to the *Times* of March 26, 1910, by the military correspondent of that journal, whom I had respectfully reproached with having abandoned his old hostility to shock. Cavalry patrols, unless they are to be "trussed chickens," must, he now said, have lances and swords in order, *inter alia*, to be able, when meeting other Cavalry patrols "in villages and lanes, or at the corner of some wood," to "tear the eyes out of" them! These "Œdipean evulsions" form a picturesque improvement even on von Bernhardi's "rude force," and strike a decidedly happier note than the patrol "charging after due reflection." But why, I asked, could not the act be performed on even one single occasion in three years of war in South Africa? Why not in one single recorded case in a year's war in Manchuria? Well, one must admit that the "corner of the wood" was an ingenious touch. It suggested a close, blind, wooded district of England, so prohibitive of shock in large bodies and for that reason so unlike South Africa and Manchuria. Yet there were many similar obstacles in both those regions: there were hundreds of villages; there were hills, mountains, ravines, dongas, sharp rocky ridges, river-beds, clumps of bush and trees, farm buildings; there were the great tracts of bush-veldt in the Transvaal, the tall millet of Northern Manchuria, and so on—quite enough, certainly, to lead to the tearing out of the eyes of at least one careless scout or patrol. Colonel Repington knows these facts as well as I do, and once more, in view of his great—and deservedly great—influence on contemporary thought, I beg him to return to his earlier manner, and speak once more in his old slashing style about the futility of "classic charges and prehistoric methods." After all, this is the very language used by von Bernhardi, whom, in the letter I have been alluding to, Colonel Repington described as a "very eminent authority."

I have the letter before me, and it is with a somewhat grim satisfaction that I observe the Nemesis which overtakes publicists who are rash enough to recant opinions founded on national experience and confirmed by the most recent facts of war. It was written just before von Bernhardi's book was published, and a large part of it took the form of an eulogy on the German Cavalry, whom he defended hotly from my charge of "sentimental conservatism," whose new regulations about fire-action he quoted with admiring approval, and whose revivification he distinctly associated with the name of that "very eminent authority" General von Bernhardi. The very eminent authority spoke a few weeks later, and said that his "writings had fallen on barren soil." His language about the sentimental conservatism of the present German Cavalry beggared any I had used. He made his own Colonel Repington's epithet "prehistoric"; his phrase "old-fashioned knightly combats" is surely an

130

adequate counterpart to "classic charges"; in many a passage of biting invective he deplores as literal truth at the present moment what Colonel Repington scouted as a libellous myth invented by me—namely, that in peace manœuvres "solid lines of steel-clad Cavalry are led across open plains"; and, as I have shown, he regards as utterly unprepared for war a Cavalry which Colonel Repington holds up as an example to his British readers of "the best modern Cavalries," and which, if we do not imitate their methods, would, he thinks, in the event of a war, tear the eyes out of ours. As to fire-action, perhaps Colonel Repington had not studied the German Regulations with a very critical eye before he praised them to the point of asking, "Could Botha or Delarey or De Wet ask for more?" In the light of von Bernhardi's strictures and of his still stranger alternatives, the topic, I am sure, will need different handling if Colonel Repington returns to it.

Finally, I repeat once more that, for Englishmen, one of the best practical criteria of the steel theory, in regard both to reconnaissance and battle functions, lies in the existence of our Mounted Infantry force. Their revised Manual (1909), reticent and incomplete as it is sometimes in the interests of the sacred shock theory, is, in effect, a crushing indictment of that theory. They are trained to do precisely the same work as the Cavalry. They are not only to act as purely divisional mounted troops, but, like the German divisional Cavalry, are intended to co-operate with and, in circumstances which must constantly happen, act as substitutes for the Independent Cavalry. This is criminal folly if, from the lack of a sword or lance, they are "trussed chickens," whose morale, in the words of Colonel Repington, will be "destroyed" by steel-armed Cavalry. Thank Heaven, they listen with indifference to this language—language which would indeed be calculated to destroy the morale of any force with less self-respect and less splendid war traditions behind it. They know in their hearts that their methods are in reality not despised but feared by Continental Cavalry, for the reasons frankly and honestly set forth by General von Bernhardi. Their leaders now are the sole official repositories of what is really our great national tradition for mounted troops in civilized war; for the steel tradition is a legend dating from Balaclava, a battle which is scarcely more relevant to modern needs than Crécy —and Crécy, by the way, was one of the greatest of all the historic triumphs of missile weapons over shock. It was not the lack of swords and lances, but the possession of swords and lances, which tended to turn men into "trussed chickens" in South Africa and Manchuria. It was the rifle in both cases which made Cavalry mobile and formidable. It is melancholy to think that our true principles and sound traditions of mounted warfare are embodied in so small a force, organized on such an illogical system, provided with a training of altogether inadequate length, and hampered by nominal subservience to a steel-armed Cavalry whose theories of action have been proved in two long and bloody wars to be obsolete.

It is perhaps even more melancholy to see so many Yeomanry officers agitating for an opportunity to ape the worst features of the Cavalry, while neglecting the best features of the very force whose exact tactical counterpart they are; dreaming sentimental nonsense about Bredow's charge at Vionville, while under their eyes lie the pitiless records of idleness and failure on the part of those whose aim it was to imitate Bredow, and the still sadder story of the penalties paid in South Africa for inexperience in the rifle by the Yeomanry themselves.

I sometimes wonder if Houndsditch will open the eyes of the public to the unrealities of Cavalry manœuvre. How many

132

Cavalry, *condemned to remain in their saddles,* would it take to disable or capture a patrol of determined men using automatic pistols (to say nothing of magazine rifles) either in a "village or lane or at the corner of some wood," or on the rolling downs of Salisbury or Lambourne?

FOOTNOTES:

[5] See "Cavalry Training," p. 194. "It will thus gain freedom to carry out its ultimate rôle of reconnaissance." See also p. 196, where the principle is repeated with emphasis, an exception being made in favour of the case where the enemy's Cavalry is outside the zone of operations!

[6] Yet on page 190 he contrasts action *en masse* in the battle of all Arms with previous action "in detail."

CHAPTER IX

THE RIFLE RULES TACTICS

("*Die Feuerwaffe beherrscht die Taktik*")

I.—GENERAL VON BERNHARDI ON SOUTH AFRICA.

"THE rifle (or literally, the firearm) rules tactics." The phrase was originally my own, but the General has done me the honour of adopting and sanctioning it, and I may fitly bring this criticism of his writings to a conclusion by briefly noting the occasion and origin of this remarkable admission. My book, "War and the *Arme Blanche*," was published in March, 1910, a month before the publication in England of his own second work, "Cavalry in War and Peace," whose consideration we have just concluded. In the course of the summer of 1910 the General published a series of articles in the *Militär Wochenblatt* criticizing my book, and those articles were translated and printed in the *Cavalry Journal* of October, 1910.

The critic covers limited ground. He makes no rejoinder or allusion of any sort to my own chapter of detailed criticism upon his own earlier work, "Cavalry in Future Wars." He scarcely notices my discussion of the Manchurian War. He confines himself almost wholly to the South African War, and makes it plain (1) that his knowledge of that war is exceedingly deficient; (2) that his principal explanation for the comparative failure of our Regular Cavalry in that war was that they were timidly led; (3) that he had misunderstood the nature of the case which I had endeavoured to construct against the *arme blanche*, and that, so far as he did understand it, he agreed with my conclusions.

1. Internal evidence shows—what one would naturally infer from the extraordinary conceptions of the technique of fire-action for mounted troops developed in his book—that the General[7] has never studied closely the combats of our war, except, perhaps, in such publications as the German Official History, which leaves off at March, 1900, practically ignores the mounted question, regards the Boers throughout as Infantry (presumably because, though mounted, they did not carry lances and swords), and, as a result of this method of exposition, is of no value towards the present controversy. Unfamiliar with the phenomena of our war, the General nevertheless taunts me, who argued solely from the facts of war and went not an inch beyond the facts, with being a "speculative theorist"—a taunt which comes strangely from an author who declares in his current volume (p. 7) that "the groundwork of training" for modern Cavalry can only be created from "speculative and theoretical reflection." He proceeds further to obliterate my humble personality by remarking that I am "naturally devoid of all war experience," and that he would never have taken the trouble to discuss the subject at all if Lord Roberts had not declared his agreement with what I had written. The personal point, of course, is wholly immaterial, and I welcome his perfectly correct choice of an opponent. But his

spontaneous allusion to war experience raises a somewhat important point. Until reading the words, I had never dreamed that my own war experience was a serious factor in the discussion. I have never alluded to it or argued from it; but since the point is raised, let me say to General von Bernhardi that, in common with some hundreds of thousands of my countrymen here or in the Colonies, I have had, in a very humble capacity, a certain kind of war experience, of which he, as a reflective theorist, stands in bitter need. We have *seen* the modern rifle at work in what he calls "real war." We have *seen* what he has only reflected about and imagined—the revolution wrought by it on the battle-field since the days of 1870. He has not; and if he had, he would have avoided many of the painful solecisms and blunders which disfigure his work, enlightened as that work is by comparison with the retrograde school he attacks.

2. TIMID LEADING. —The Boers, says the General, were a "peasant militia," who were "tied to their ox-waggons," "incapable of assuming the offensive on a large scale," in "disappearing smaller numbers against greatly superior numbers," "not often strong enough either to charge the English Cavalry or to attack the English Infantry," "directed by halting leadership," and so on—altogether, according to the General's standards, a most contemptible foe, hardly worthy of the steel of a respectable professional Cavalry, and certainly not the kind of foe to force such a Cavalry to abandon its traditional form of combat. But there was the rub. Our Cavalry, it seems, was even more contemptible. They "made no relentless pursuits, despite the lack of operative mobility in the enemy"; "they did not attack even when they had the opportunity"; and "one could scarcely find a European Cavalry which was tied down to such an extent during the big operations as the Boers, or one which,

against such little resistance, did not try to overcome it as the English." He cites the action of Dronfield,[8] where Sir John French was in command, as a specific instance, and in as plain language as it is possible to use without penning the word "cowardice," accuses the Cavalry present of that unpardonable crime. "Mr. Childers," he remarks with perfect truth, "relates the story without any spite to show the little value of English Cavalry equipment and training. *I think it shows much beside.*"[9] (The italics are mine.)

I do not know if this kind of thing will finally compel Sir John French to examine more thoroughly the foundations of his own belief in the lance and sword, and to apply more searching criticism to the works of the "acknowledged authority" whom he lauds to the skies as a model and Mentor for British Cavalrymen. I should hope that, on their behalf, he now resents as hotly as I resent the contemptuous patronage of an officer holding and expressing the view that "any European Cavalry"—and he afterwards expressly names the German Cavalry—would have shown more aggressive spirit in South Africa than our own—more aggressive spirit, be it understood, *with the lance and sword*; for if that be not the meaning, the General's lengthy appreciation of the worth and exploits of the rival forces in South Africa is, in its context, as part of a hostile criticism of my work, either destructive of his own argument or meaningless. Sir John French refuses to read through British eyes the plain moral of the war for Cavalry. This is his reward, and it is of no use to pretend that he does not deserve it. Anyone who throws the dearly-bought experience of his own countrymen to the winds, and runs to foreigners who have no relevant experience for corroboration of an outworn creed, gratuitously courts the same humiliation.

Perhaps I make too much of a point of pride. Let Sir John

French at any rate see the amusing side of the situation. He has set forth[10] his own four reasons for the failure of the lance and sword in South Africa: (1) The lightning speed of the Boers in running away from combat—a habit which left our Cavalry nothing even to reconnoitre; (2) the fact that our military object was nothing less than the complete conquest and annexation of the enemy's country; (3) that, owing to the release of prisoners who fought again against us, we had to contend with double the number of men nominally allowed for; (4) the condition of the horses.

The last factor the German author does not pretend to take seriously as an explanation of the failure of the Cavalry; and with regard to the first three his view, as far as it receives clear expression, is diametrically the reverse of that of Sir John French. So far from alleging that the Boers "dispersed for hundreds of miles when pressed," he dwells repeatedly on the immobility imposed by their ox-waggons, says that they were "tied down" to an unparalleled extent, and censures the Cavalry for what he regards as their unparalleled slackness in attack against such a vulnerable and unenterprising enemy. So far from agreeing that there was "nothing to reconnoitre," he points out that the Cavalry "did not understand reconnaissance by Cavalry patrols," a statement true enough in itself, but valueless without the reason—namely, the mistaken armament and training of the Cavalry—a reason which would, of course, have applied with infinitely greater force to "any other European Cavalry," because no Cavalry but our own would have had the invaluable assistance of Colonial mounted riflemen, armed and trained correctly. So far from finding an excuse for the failure of the lance and sword in the fact that our aim was conquest and annexation, he appears in the last page of his article to argue that, had these weapons been used more "relentlessly," the British nation would not now be in what he evidently regards as the degrading situation of having Boers on a footing of political equality with British citizens! Finally, so far from pleading the abnormal accretions to the Boer Army through the release of captured prisoners, he makes a particular point of our vast numerical superiority and of the "disappearing smaller numbers" of the enemy.

But the climax comes when he coolly tells Sir John French that the German Cavalry, whose backwardness and "indolence" he condemns in the very book which Sir John French sponsors, whom he regards as absolutely "unprepared for war," whose "prehistoric" tactics, "old-fashioned knightly combats," "antiquated Regulations," and "tactical orgies," he is at this moment satirizing, would, twelve years ago, with still more antiquated Regulations, with still less education, and with a far worse armament, have taught the Boer peasants lessons with the steel which our faint-spirited Cavalry could not teach them! All patriotic feelings apart, and merely as a military experiment, one would like to have seen the German Uhlans of 1899, with their popgun carbine and Frederician traditions, and without a vestige of aid, inspiration or example from Colonial or Mounted Infantry sources, tackling the Boers at Talana or Zand River, at Colenso, Diamond Hill, or Magersfontein, at Ladysmith or Sannah's Post, at Roodewal or Bakenlaagte. At the last two episodes the General is quite certain that they would have done far more marvellous feats with the steel by means of an old-fashioned knightly combat than the Boers did with the rifle.

Serious students of land-war, anxious only to elucidate the purely technical question as to whether horsemen in modern days can fight effectively on horseback with steel weapons, look on in amazed bewilderment, while high authorities on the affirmative side conspire to render themselves and one another ridiculous by dragging in political, psychological, strategical, and even lyrical factors which have nothing whatever to do with the simple issue of combat. There, as I have often said, is the reader's clue through the labyrinth of contradictions. Neither Sir John French nor General von Bernhardi ever really discusses at all the real point at issue. That is why they succeed in agreeing upon it, while differing radically in their logical processes. As the reader probably realizes now, nearly everything the latter General writes is either susceptible of two constructions or is subject to subsequent qualification. This critical essay on the opinions of Lord Roberts and on my book, "War and the *Arme Blanche*," is only another illustration of the same mental habit. Though he is explicit enough on what he regards as the feeble initiative of the British Army in general and the British Cavalry in particular, he never attempts to trace any direct causal connection between this topic and the topic of the lance or sword. He dare not. Remote insinuation is his only weapon. Yet, for the purposes of his article, that specific link is the only thing worth talking about. So far as he does touch the question of physical combat—as, for example, where he says that the Boers "fought entirely with the rifle, and this the mounted troops of England had to learn," "that the Boers were far superior in the fire-fight," that the absence of "Cavalry duels" in South Africa was caused (mark this deliciously naïve admission) by the fact of the armament and the numerical weakness of the Boers—he is on my side. And I need scarcely add that the reader will find it easy to demolish the General's whole dream of the lost opportunities of the lance and sword in South Africa or Manchuria, or of its golden chances in any future war, by passages from the General's own work, criticized in this volume, as when he implores his own Cavalry to remember that they may have to meet mounted riflemen, or even heterodox Cavalry, who, using their horses only as a means of mobility in the Boer fashion, will, in defiance of the German text-books, advance dismounted, and force the German troopers to do the same; or when he lays down that the attack or defence of any "locality," entrenched or unentrenched, and by whomsoever defended or attacked, must be accomplished through fire-action. It is true that the theoretical limitations he sets to fire-action, from sheer ignorance of what fire-action by mounted troops is, reduce that form of combat also to a nullity; but on that point anyone can test his views by facts. Although it is quite possible to prove from his premisses, if their truth be postulated, that the South African War never took place at all, without going to the trouble of proving that it was "abnormal" in the matter of the futility of the lance and sword, we know that it did take place, why lances and swords were futile, and why fire was supreme.

3. So in reality does General von Bernhardi himself, and in the title of this chapter is crystallized his explicit statement of the truth. Faithful to his habitual system of alternate adhesion to two incompatible theories, the General, after clearly enough condemning the British Cavalry for their timidity with the steel, makes the following remarkable *volte face*:

> "In one particular, however, I will own he [*i.e.,* Mr. Childers] is correct: the firearm rules tactics. That is indisputable. Nobody can with the *arme blanche* compel an opponent on his side tactically to use the *arme blanche*." (This last is a very dark saying, for the Boers had no *arme blanche*; but it does not affect the general sense.) "To the laws of the fire-fight everything must be subordinated in war."

Well, that is precisely what Lord Roberts, the greatest soldier living, and many humbler persons, including myself, have contended for. *Cadit quæstio.* Why not have begun "Cavalry in War and Peace" with these illuminating axioms? Why not have them placed in the forefront of our own Cavalry Manual, in the approaching revision of that important work? Why give the dominating operative weapon only 10 or 15 per cent. of the time of the Cavalry soldier, and make it officially subordinate to steel weapons which can only be used by its indulgence? But I am going a little too fast. The General, as usual, has a qualification. What is it? "But as a necessary corollary from this, to say that there can be no fight with the *arme blanche* is a mischievous sophism." Again we agree—in the sense, that is, in which the author now elects to use the phrase *"arme blanche."* For he means the bayonet. "Every Infantryman carries a bayonet, because he requires it for the assault. Even Lord Roberts will not take this away," etc. No; and no one in the world, so far as I know, wants to take away the bayonet from the Infantryman. But, as I asked at page 121, what has the bayonet got to do with the lance and sword? The bayonet is fixed to the rifle, and used on foot as an element in fire-tactics. The lance and sword are used from horseback in tactics which are diametrically opposite to and absolutely incompatible with fire-tactics, and every word Lord Roberts or I have written has been directly aimed against this antiquated system of fighting on horseback with the lance and sword. If the Cavalryman, because, by universal consent, he has constantly to do work similar to that of Infantry, requires a bayonet, by all means give it to him. I discussed the question in my previous book, and ventured to regard it as an open one, for reasons which I need not repeat now. But I over and over again took pains to point out the fundamental distinction between the bayonet and the lance and sword.

On another point the General misrepresents me. Because I showed by illustration from war the marked physical and moral effects of rifle-fire from the saddle, he treats me as advancing the specific plan of substituting rifle-fire on horseback for the use of the lance and sword on horseback in what his translator calls the "collision of the mounted fight" (Handgemenge zu Pferde). This is a perversion of my meaning. The collisions he is thinking of are obsolete. Though I think that for all conceivable purposes a pistol would be better than a lance or sword, I adhered to the facts, and pointed out that saddle-fire in South Africa was used *before* contact, and that in order to consummate their destructive rifle-charges, the Boers dismounted, either at close quarters or within point-blank range.

II. — *Views of the General Staff.*

I wish to lay special stress on these two misrepresentations, because both have been also made by our own General Staff. In a review of my previous book, whose general fairness and courtesy I gladly recognize, the *Monthly Notes* of July, 1910, took exactly the same erroneous points, and, for the rest, adopted the strange course of ruling out all the remarkable South African charges with the rifle by quietly assuming that they would have been done better with the sword or lance.

He takes as an example the action of Bakenlaagte, and convinces himself that Cavalry "as ably led" would, by sticking persistently to their saddles, have done better with the steel than the Boers who inflicted such terrible punishment with their rifles upon Benson's brave and seasoned troops. This is an unintentional slur not only upon Benson's men but upon our Cavalry, who, on the reviewer's assumption, ought certainly to have inflicted similar punishment upon the Boers on scores of occasions where the tactical conditions were approximately the same

143

as those at Bakenlaagte. The reviewer arbitrarily begins his imaginary parallel at the moment at which Botha's final charge started, and pictures the steel-trained troops already in full career like the fire-trained troops who actually made the charge. War is not so easy as all that. He ignores the characteristically clever fire-tactics which for hours before had been leading up to the requisite situation, and forgets that steel-trained troops would never have had the skill or insight to produce and utilize that situation. Moreover, their training Manual not only does not contemplate, but renders prohibitive any such instantaneous transition from fire to shock as would have been required. But the reviewer surpasses himself when, having triumphantly brought his steel-trained troops through the preparatory phase and the charging phase (with the incidental riding down and capture of several detached bodies of men), he pictures them confronted with the objective ultimately charged—namely, Benson's rearguard of guns and riflemen on Gun Hill. These men had had just time to rally, and were lined out on a long ridge in open order and in splendid fighting fettle. Their fire hitherto had been masked by the rearmost sections of their own men, who were galloping in with the Boers at their heels. What the Boers now did was to fling themselves from their ponies, by instinct, in the dead ground below the ridge, and to charge up it on foot, where after a brief and desperate encounter they exterminated Benson's heroic rearguard and captured the guns. This action the reviewer regards as clumsy and dilatory. His Lancers, disdaining to dismount, would have ridden up the hill—painfully vulnerable targets for the rifles on the ridge—and, arrived on the top, would either have gone riding about among the scattered defenders trying to impale with lances or reach with swords riflemen who would have laughed in their faces at this ineffectual method of fighting, or (and the reviewer favours this alternative) would have been content to impale a chance few *en passant*, and, without drawing rein, would have galloped on towards the main body and convoy, leaving "supporting squadrons," whom he coolly invents for the occasion (for the Boers had none), to "deal with" the rearguard in the knightly fashion aforesaid. Sweeping on, and again disdaining to dismount on reaching the next objective, our Lancers would have "spread havoc and consternation" among the convoy. Would they? You cannot stampede or disable inspanned oxen and mules or their drivers by brandishing swords and lances. And surely one does not "charge" ox-waggons with those weapons. What you want for these occasions is the bullet, whether for beasts, drivers, or escort. By bitter experience of our own on only too many occasions we know all about the right way of spreading havoc and consternation among convoys. Lances and swords never produced these effects in a single case in three years. And the escort and main body? Why, a few dozen steady men with rifles would turn the tables on, and, in their turn, spread havoc among a whole brigade of Lancers who insisted on remaining in their saddles.

One falls, I must frankly admit, into profound discouragement when one meets arguments of this sort coming from a quarter where arguments lead to rules and regulations. It is quite true that this important review, in its moderate tone and in its tacit avowal that there was need of some reform in the present regulations, bore no resemblance to the criticisms which proceeded from some individual Cavalry officers. There were indications—reliable, I hope— that the old knee-to-knee knightly shock-charge, now regarded officially as the "climax of Cavalry training," was doomed, and that the open-order charge with the steel, presumed to be analogous to the open-order charge with the rifle, was the utmost now contemplated. But in truth, as

I pointed out in Chapters IV. and VI., there exists no such analogy, or the war would have demonstrated it. If such steel-charges were possible, our Cavalry had innumerable chances of carrying them out under far more favourable conditions, owing to our permanent numerical superiority, than the Boers ever obtained for their attacks, by the charge or otherwise.

The steel-charge, close or open, was the traditional function of our Cavalry; it was the only form of combat that they really understood when they landed in South Africa, and they were supremely efficient in it. The point is that in practice they *could* not charge with the steel, except in the rare and well-nigh negligible cases which are on record. They ceased altogether to try so to charge, because to fight with the steel on horseback was physically impossible. Their steel weapons were eventually returned to store on that account. And they profited by the resulting change of spirit, and by the acquisition, late as it came, of a respectable firearm. To say that the fire-charge invented and practised by the Boers as early as March, 1900, when lances and swords were still in the field, and imitated to some extent by our own Colonials and Mounted Infantry, could, after all, have been done as well and better with the lance and sword, is conjecture run mad. Sir John French has never used the argument. He could not, with any shadow of plausibility, combine it with his complaint about the lightning flights of the Boers and the absence of anything to reconnoitre. It is, I grant, the most impressive official testimonial ever given to the *arme blanche*, but it is not business. One might as well argue that the work done by Togo's torpedo-boats would have been done better by the beaks of triremes. We *know and have seen* what actually happened. We had nearly three years in which to arrive by experiment at tactical truths. In the name of common sense let us accept the results, especially when they are corroborated by the results of the other great modern war, that in Manchuria.

III.—Other Cavalry Views.

Directly or indirectly, I think that in the course of this volume I have replied to most of the criticisms which my previous book, "War and the *Arme Blanche*," drew forth. But I should like to make a brief reference to an interesting discussion of the subject conducted mainly by Cavalry officers on October 19, 1910, at the Royal United Service Institution. A reader of the report in the *Journal* of November, 1910, must feel that the proceedings would have gained in clarity and harmony had von Bernhardi's belated maxim that the "firearm rules tactics" been made the basis of the debate. Strange things were said on the side of the *arme blanche*. One officer urged that Cavalry should not have a rifle—that arbiter of tactics—at all, should use shock alone, and should not be "frittered away as scouts." Another complained that, in arguing mainly from the South African and Manchurian Wars, I "could not have selected two worse examples." I am not to blame. It is not a case of selection. These are the *only* great civilized wars since the "revolution" (to use von Bernhardi's phrase) wrought by modern firearms.

The close-order shock-charge has never even been tried or contemplated in civilized war since 1870, and even then it was moribund. Yet the lecturer argued from Waterloo, and, unconscious of the slight upon his Arm, was at great pains to claim that even now Cavalry kept in reserve for the occasion could attack two-year conscripts who had already been reduced to "pulp" by several days of fire and fatigue. "*If,*" he said, "they could stick their lances into quite a large proportion," the rest "would have the most marked reluctance to remain upon the ground." Perhaps. Von

Bernhardi also claims that Infantry, who under stress of fire have reached the point of throwing away their arms, may be attacked successfully with the steel. Let us allow the claim, only remarking that experience shows a rifle to be a far more destructive weapon for such circumstances than a lance or sword. But, instead of idly awaiting these not very glorious opportunities for the steel, would it not be better for the Cavalry to be mobile and busy from the first in using the same formidable weapon which originally reduced the Infantry to pulp, using it in that limitless sphere of envelopment, interception, and surprise to which the possession of horses gives them access?

Another extraordinary feature of the discussion was the dissociation of moral effect from killing effect by some of the Cavalry officers present, who really seemed to think that riflemen in war are afraid of horses, irrespective of weapons, whereas in fact they welcome so substantial a target for their rifles, and fear only the rider's weapon *in direct proportion to its deadliness*. These officers were convinced that their Arm, trained to charge as it now is, exercises great moral effect, yet they agreed that the importance of killing the enemy with the steel is at present neglected, and that the art of so killing is not even taught. The lecturer argued that our Cavalry would be a "more terrifying weapon than it is at present" if every trooper could be brought to "understand that he has to stick his sword or lance into the body of his opponent." Another officer urged that "each horseman in a charge should be taught that he must kill at least one adversary"; and the Chairman strongly emphasized "the necessity of training the men to kill." "The reason," he said, "that a man had a sword or spear was to kill." The truth is that some arts perish from disuse. This art cannot be exercised in war, so wars come and go, and the very tradition of its exercise disappears, and in peace is replaced, as the Chairman said, by "piercing yells" and the "waving of swords."

A Horse Artillery officer threw a bombshell into the debate by complaining that his Arm was often forbidden at manœuvres to open fire on the hostile Cavalry masses (*vide supra*, pp. 127 and 131), in order to allow the collision to take place on "favourable ground," and asked for guidance. The Chairman replied that the Artillery could be trusted to be "loyal." But can they, in this particular matter? Let us hope not.

A small minority ably upheld the case against the *arme blanche*, and the discussion, as a whole, was of considerable value. General Sir R.S. Baden-Powell went to the root of the matter when he confessed that a "policy had never properly been laid down" for the Cavalry, and that they "wanted a policy to begin with before they commenced training." That is the literal truth, and I hope to have proved that no rational, clear, consistent policy ever will be laid down until the rifle is made in peace-theory what it already is in war-practice—the dominant, all-important weapon of Cavalry—and until the axiom that the rifle rules tactics is accepted and systematically acted upon. I claim that von Bernhardi's writings, and the manner of their acceptance in this country, prove conclusively that that is the condition precedent to a sound policy. He has no policy; we have no policy. We have not even a terminology suitable to modern conditions.

I believe it correct also to say that the principal cause of the persistence of the *arme blanche* theory in this country is its retention by foreign Cavalries who are without war experience, and who, on account of its retention, are backward in every department of their science.

In Sir John French's words, we try to assimilate the best

foreign customs, and we choose for assimilation the very customs which we ourselves have proved in war to be not only valueless, but vicious.

I have not thought it worth while to deal with other Continental Cavalries. In the matter of the lance and sword, the Austrian and French Cavalries may be regarded as more backward than the German. Both would regard von Bernhardi as a fanatical heretic. Count Wrangel, for the Austrians, states that it is impossible to train Cavalry to the use of two weapons so different as the sword and the rifle, and, in deciding for the former, frankly admits that, after the experience of Manchuria, Cavalry have no business within the zone of fire. The views and practice of the French Cavalry may be learnt from the scathing exposure to which they have been submitted by General de Négrier. Our Cavalry, excessive as its reliance on the steel is, stands, of course, in the matter of fire-action, ahead of all Continental rivals.

Relying too much on foreign practice in peace, we also exaggerate foreign exploits in bygone wars where conditions were radically different. I scarcely think it too much to say, after a close study of the criticisms of my book, that, if one could only succeed in proving to present-day Cavalrymen that von Bredow's charge at Vionville was not a valid precedent for modern war, more than half the battle for rational armament and tactics would be won. Quite half my critics threw that famous charge in my teeth, and some accused me of not even knowing about it, since I had not mentioned it. Why should I have mentioned it? I was not aware at the time I wrote that it was seriously accepted as relevant to present conditions. Von Bernhardi, whom I was taking as a representative of the most enlightened Cavalry views on the subject of the steel-charge, does not mention it in either of his works, and in his first work went to some trouble to show how the German and French Cavalry at Mars-la-Tour frittered away time and opportunity by hanging about in masses which "mutually paralyzed" one another, instead of using golden chances for fire-action. He expressly says that the war of 1870 "presents a total absence of analogy," and, as I showed above (p. 140), his own limitations for the steel-charge in modern war absolutely preclude the possibility of any such charge being repeated. Those limitations have for long been accepted by Cavalry in this country also—in theory. But the immortal fascination of that charge! Next door to von Bernhardi's article on my book in the *Cavalry Journal* of October, 1910, is an interesting descriptive account of it, with maps. And the author ends thus: "The days of Cavalry are not over. For they 'can ride rapidly into the danger that Infantry can only walk into.'" These two little sentences typify perfectly, I believe, the state of mind of those who cling to the *arme blanche* out of sentiment and without scientific justification. Nobody supposes that the days of Cavalry are over. Far from being weakened, Cavalry, if properly equipped and trained, have potentialities immensely greater than the Cavalry of 1870, because they now possess—in our country at any rate—the weapon which, united with the horse, qualifies them to tackle any other Arm on their own terms. And as the writer of this article truly says, they can ride into the danger that Infantry can only walk into. South Africa proves that, to a certain point. But, alas! that is not the moral that the writer means to draw. He forgets that the rifle of 1870 is, as I remarked before, a museum curiosity, and that, feeble as it was, it nearly cut to pieces Bredow's regiments on their return from the charge. He draws the wrong moral—that Cavalry can still make charges by remaining indefinitely in their saddles and wielding steel weapons from their saddles. In that sense the days of Cavalry are indeed over. Nobody should regret it. What is there to regret?

151

But let me repeat one last caution. It is a harmful result of this otherwise healthy controversy that we tend to argue too much in terms of the "charge," meaning the mounted charge, culminating in a fight at close quarters, or even in a mêlée. For all we know, future science, by making it a sheer impossibility to get so large an object as a horse through a fire-zone, may eventually render such an attack by horsemen, in whatever formation and with whatever weapon, altogether impracticable. What will there be to regret in that? Sailors do not mourn over the decay of the cutlass and the ram. *So long as we win*, it does not matter whether or not we charge on horseback, or how near we can ride to the objective before we begin the fire-fight. And, come what will, the horse, by the correct use of ground and surprise, will always be a priceless engine of strategical and tactical mobility.

FOOTNOTES:

[7] Note, for example, his reiteration of the phrase, whose falsity anyone can demonstrate, that the Boers showed "no offensive power," with the implied inference, never explicitly worked out, but left in the realm of vague insinuation, that this failure was in some way connected with their lack of lances and swords, weapons which they would not have taken at a gift, and could not have used if they had had them.

[8] See "War and the *Arme Blanche*," pp. 113-115.

[9] Conscious, apparently, of the gross personal discourtesy to Sir John French, he adds that "since General French was there, lack of energy cannot be imputed to the attack." This not only stultifies what precedes, but is untrue. The attack was painfully unenergetic; nobody has denied it. The point is that the lack of energy was due to the fact that the Cavalry were not armed and trained for such an occasion. Of their three weapons, two, the lance and the sword, were useless, and the third was a trumpery little carbine, which in peace theory had been regarded as an almost negligible part of their equipment. What they needed was the fire-spirit, a serious firearm, and

training in mobile fire-tactics.

[10] See *supra*, pp. 17-27.

CHAPTER X

THE MORAL

THE moral is simple and inspiring—self-reliance, trust in our own experience, as confirmed by the subsequent experience of others. By all means let us borrow what is good from foreigners, and I should be the last to deny that, on topics unconnected with combat and weapons, there are many valuable hints to be obtained from General von Bernhardi's writings, and those of other foreign Cavalrymen. But let us not borrow what is bad, nor lose ourselves in the fog which smothers his Cavalry principles, when our own road to reform is plain.

Some measure of reform, if report is true, is to take shape in the next revision of the Cavalry Manual. I end, as I began, with expressing the hope that reform may be drastic. But reform cannot end with the Cavalry Manual. It is absolutely necessary to introduce clearness, consistency and harmony into the four Manuals: "Cavalry Training" (with its absurd postscript for Yeomanry), "Mounted Infantry Training," "Infantry Training," and "Combined Training." At present the contradictions between these official Manuals is a public scandal. But I suggest that the task of reconstruction is absolutely impossible unless the basis taken be that fire, by whomsoever employed, is absolute arbiter of tactics, and that the Cavalryman is for practical purposes a compound of three factors—man, horse, and rifle.

The lance should go altogether. Whether the sword is retained, as the American Cavalry retain it, rather as a symbol than as a factor in tactics, or is dispensed with altogether, as our divisional mounted troops and our Colonial mounted riflemen dispense with it, is a matter of very small moment, provided that the correct principle be established and worked out in practice. It was because I doubted the possibility of establishing the correct principle in this country without abolition that in my previous book I advocated abolition, on the precedent of the South African War. The adoption of a bayonet or a sword-bayonet is, in my own humble opinion, an interesting open question.

THE END

BILLING AND SONS, LTD., PRINTERS, GUILDFORD

ADVERTISEMENTS

SELECTIONS FROM

MR. EDWARD ARNOLD'S LIST OF NEW AND RECENT

BOOKS.

UNEXPLORED SPAIN.

By ABEL CHAPMAN,

Author of "Bird-Life of the Borders," "Wild Norway," "On Safari";

And WALTER J. BUCK,

British Vice-Consul at Jerez.

With more than 200 Illustrations from Drawings by the Authors, Joseph Crawhall, and others, and from Photographs, including some by H.R.H. Philippe, Duke of Orleans. 1 Volume super-royal 8vo., 21s. net.

"A very striking volume, full of good things from cover to cover; and illustrations well worthy of the text."—*Illustrated London News.*

"'Wild Spain,' produced by the same authors in 1892, seemed to leave little room for this volume, but riper experience, a wider survey, and keener analysis have brought justification for the hopes engendered by the praise accorded to the earlier work. Moreover, the previous book gives an added interest to this one, and a faith in its authors that will enable readers to accept, without pause, statements which might otherwise cause a little hesitation, for it must come as a surprise to some when they are told that in Spain there are wildfowl by the million, wild camels, and wild men. The numerous illustrations, which have been perseveringly sought, are excellent, and add to the charm of this fascinating book."—*Daily Chronicle.*

"Every sportsman and naturalist who reads it will be

grateful for one of the best works of the kind published in recent years."—*Daily Graphic*.

———————————————————————

LONDON: EDWARD ARNOLD, 41 & 43 MADDOX STREET, W.

THE END OF THE IRISH PARLIAMENT.

By JOSEPH R. FISHER, B.A.,

Author of "Finland and the Tsars."

Demy 8vo., 10s. 6d. net.

The period dealt with by the Author comprises the last thirty years of the Irish Parliament. The system of Dual Government—that "vulture gnawing at the vitals of the Empire," as Lord Rosebery has called it—was then on its trial. It had already broken down in Scotland, and in Ireland the irrepressible conflict between closer union on the one hand and complete separation on the other went steadily on to its destined end.

The crisis came when England found herself at war; a French invasion of Ireland was attempted, and a fierce Rebellion broke out. The causes that led to this Rebellion, its failure, Pitt's decision that only in complete Union could a remedy be found for the desperate evils of the country, and the means by which the Union was carried, constitute an important chapter in Irish history, and one not without its bearing on current problems.

GERMAN INFLUENCE ON BRITISH CAVALRY.

By ERSKINE CHILDERS,

Author of "War and the Arme Blanche," "The Riddle of the Sands"; Editor of Vol. V. of "'The Times' History of the War

Crown 8vo., 3s. 6d. net.

In the course of the keen and widespread controversy aroused by the Author's book, "War and the Arme Blanche," published last year with an introduction by Field-Marshal Lord Roberts, it became clear that foreign influence—and especially German influence—was the principal cause of our adherence to the obsolete tactics based on the lance and sword. This impression has been confirmed by the recent appearance of a translation of General von Bernhardi's latest work, "Cavalry in War and Peace," with a commendatory preface from the pen of General Sir John French, our foremost cavalry authority. No modern work of this same scale and character, by a British cavalry writer, exists, and it is this work, therefore, which Mr. Childers, in his coming volume, "German Influence on British Cavalry," submits to close analysis and criticism.

THE LIFE OF THE RIGHT HON. CECIL JOHN RHODES.

By the HON. SIR LEWIS MICHELL,

MEMBER OF THE EXECUTIVE COUNCIL, CAPE COLONY.

2 Volumes, Illustrated, 30s. net.

"Not for many years, if ever, will Sir Lewis Michell's book be displaced as the standard Life of his friend."—Mr. E.T. COOK in the *Daily Chronicle.*

"This is the third big book on Rhodes within four months, and although the other two were not to be despised, this is the one that counts."—*Pall Mall Gazette.*

HUGH OAKELEY ARNOLD-FORSTER.

A Memoir.

By His WIFE.

With Portraits and other Illustrations. 1 Volume, 15s. net.

"Mrs. Arnold-Forster has written with perfect discretion and faultless taste. Her Memoir is a model of what such a book should be." — *Spectator.*

"Few of us, and least of all those who disagreed with him about the Army or on political questions, will not be the better for reading this admirable Memoir." — *Westminster Gazette.*

CLARA NOVELLO'S REMINISCENCES.

Compiled by her Daughter, CONTESSA VALERIA GIGLIUCCI, from the Great Singer's Manuscript Notes.

With an Introductory Memoir by A.D. COLERIDGE.

Illustrated, 10s. 6d. net.

"Clara Novello's book makes very attractive reading." — *Morning Post.*

COMPLETION OF AN IMPORTANT WORK.

A CENTURY OF EMPIRE, 1800-1900.

Volume III., 1867-1900.

By the RIGHT HON. SIR HERBERT MAXWELL, Bart.,

Author of "the Life of Wellington," etc.

With Photogravure Portraits. Demy 8vo., 14s. net.

MISS M. LOANE'S BOOKS.

The announcement of the publication of a new book by Miss Loane never fails to awaken the attention of those who study the social problems connected with poverty, and desire that the solution of those problems shall be consistent with common sense, humanity, and the preservation of that greatest of national assets — character. In Miss Loane we find the happiest combination of the qualities required for the task she has undertaken—the task of making the British people understand what should be their true attitude towards poverty.

THE COMMON GROWTH. By M. Loane. 6s.

Just Published.

AN ENGLISHMAN'S CASTLE. By M. Loane. 6s.

NEIGHBOURS AND FRIENDS.

By M. Loane. 6s.

THE QUEEN'S POOR. By M. Loane. 3s. 6d.

ACROSS THE BRIDGES.

A Study of Social Life in South London.

By ALEXANDER PATERSON. 6s.

"Across the Bridges" is a description of a poor man's life in South London, but in its main points it is also a brief survey of the whole problem of poverty.

The book demands no particular measures of reform, and clings to no social or political theory. It is rather an introduction to the whole social problem, designed for those who know little of the poor, and would be unlikely to read a specialized text-book. The writer pleads that the rich and poor must understand one another better before reform is possible.

NEW AND CHEAPER EDITION.

EIGHTEEN YEARS IN UGANDA AND EAST AFRICA.

By the RIGHT REV. A.R. TUCKER,

Bishop of Uganda.

1 Volume, with many Illustrations and a Map, 7s. 6d. net.

TRAVEL AND SPORT.

TWENTY YEARS IN THE HIMALAYA. By Major the Hon. C.G. BRUCE, M.V.O., Fifth Gurkha Rifles. With Map. Fully Illustrated. 16s. net.

"The book is interesting from start to finish."—*Athenæum.*

"A series of pen-pictures, in the terse, forcible English of the soldier, of travel and residence, of sport and exploration in those regions in circumstances which now have passed away." *Pall Mall Gazette.*

FOREST LIFE AND SPORT IN INDIA. By SAINTHILL EARDLEY-WILMOT, C.I.E., lately Inspector-General of Forests to the Indian Government; Commissioner under the Development and Road Improvement Funds Act. Fully Illustrated. Demy 8vo., 12s. 6d. net.

"It is always interesting and instructive to hear what a man has to say about his life's work; and this is doubly the case when the subject is attractive in itself, and is presented in so charming a form as Mr. Eardley-Wilmot's book. To the sportsman the first part of the book, describing work and sport in the United Provinces, will prove of absorbing interest; and it contains (Chapter IV.) what is perhaps the best description that has ever been written 'On the Habits of Tigers.' But there is not a dull page in the whole book."—*Morning Post.*

IN FORBIDDEN SEAS: Recollections of Sea-Otter-Hunting in the Kurils. By H.J. SNOW, F.R.G.S. Illustrated. Demy 8vo., 12s. 6d. net.

"Mr. Snow has opened up what is practically new ground in

the world of exploration and of sport. An extremely brightly-written account of the sport found, the adventures met with, and the dangers incurred during a series of visits to this out-of-the-way corner of the North-West Pacific."—*Morning Post.*

RECOLLECTIONS OF AN OLD MOUNTAINEER. By WALTER LARDEN. Fully Illustrated. 14s. net.

"A volume which will heartily delight true lovers of mountaineering. A book like this, genially discursive but replete with wise maxims and instructive narratives about mountain craft, is eminently readable for the right reader."—*Times.*

A GAMEKEEPER'S NOTE-BOOK. By OWEN JONES, Author of "Ten Years of Gamekeeping," and MARCUS WOODWARD. With Photogravure Illustrations. 7s. 6d. net.

"As full of pleasant reading as an egg is of meat."—*Sportsman.*

"This is a very delightful book."—*Irish Times.*

THE MISADVENTURES OF A HACK CRUISER. By F. CLAUDE KEMPSON, Author of "The *Green Finch* Cruise." With 50 Illustrations from the Author's Sketches. 6s. net.

FLY-LEAVES FROM A FISHERMAN'S DIARY. By Captain G.E. SHARP. With Photogravure Plates. 5s. net.

NEW FICTION.

THE SOUNDLESS TIDE.

By MRS. F.E. CRICHTON.

Crown 8vo., 6s.

The scene of this powerful and absorbing novel is laid in County Down, and presents a vivid picture of life among the gentry and cottagers in the North of Ireland. A strong note of passion enters into the relations of the principal characters, complicated in the case of the country-folk by the interplay of religious feeling. Whilst the tragic element is never far absent, it is not unduly dominant, for the Author has woven into her story much witty dialogue and racy portrayal of character. The atmosphere of sea air and peat-smoke seems to permeate the story and brings the persons and places very near to the reader. Mrs. Crichton has written one or two delightful stories for children, but this is her first venture into serious fiction, and it may confidently be predicted that its reception will be such as to impel her to continue in the same *genre*.

LORD BELLINGER.

An Autobiography.

With an Introduction by CAPTAIN HARRY GRAHAM,

AUTHOR OF "RUTHLESS RHYMES FOR HEARTLESS HOMES," "MISREPRESENTATIVE MEN," ETC.

Illustrated. Crown 8vo., 6s.

In his new book Captain Graham ably and amusingly satirizes the mental and moral attitude of a certain well-known section of the "leisured class." His hero, Lord Bellinger, is the very embodiment of those stolid British virtues, the possession of which ensures success, especially when unhampered by either imagination or a sense of humour. In his ingenuous autobiographical reminiscences Lord Bellinger unconsciously presents an entertaining picture of the life and doings of that portion of Society which has always offered a tempting target to the shafts of the satirist—a target of which Captain Graham takes every advantage. Readers of "Ruthless Rhymes for Heartless Homes," and Captain Graham's numerous other brilliant and frivolous works, will be interested to find him turning his talents in the direction of social satire, and will be agreeably entertained by this fresh product of his wit and observation.

FICTION.

MR. E.M. FORSTER'S GREAT NOVEL.

HOWARDS END.

By E.M. FORSTER. 6s.

"'Howards End' is packed full of good things. It stands out head and shoulders above the great mass of fiction now claiming a hearing. The autumn season has brought us some good novels, but this is, so far, the best of them."—*Daily Mail* (from a special article headed "The Season's Great Novel").

"There is no doubt about it whatever. Mr. E.M. Forster is one of the great novelists. All will agree as to the value of the book, as to its absorbing interest, the art and power with which it is put together, and they will feel with us that it is a book quite out of the common by a writer who is one of our assets, and is likely to be one of our glories."—*Daily Telegraph*.

BY THE SAME AUTHOR.

A ROOM WITH A VIEW. 6s.

THE RETURN.

By WALTER DE LA MARE. 6s.

"One of the most curiously interesting and original books that it has been our fortune to come across for a long time."—*Morning Post.*

ANNE DOUGLAS SEDGWICK'S LATEST NOVEL.

FRANKLIN KANE.

By ANNE DOUGLAS SEDGWICK,

AUTHOR OF "VALERIE UPTON," "AMABEL CHANNICE," ETC. 6s.

"A figure never to be forgotten."—*Standard.*

"There are no stereotyped patterns here."—*Daily Chronicle.*

"A very graceful and charming comedy."—*Manchester Guardian.*

A STEPSON OF THE SOIL.

By MARY J.H. SKRINE. 6s.

"Mrs. Skrine's admirable novel is one of those unfortunately rare books which, without extenuating the hard facts of life, maintain and raise one's belief in human nature. The story is simple, but the manner of its telling is admirably uncommon. Her portraits are quite extraordinarily vivid."—*Spectator.*

THE DUDLEY BOOK OF COOKERY AND HOUSEHOLD RECIPES. By GEORGIANA, COUNTESS OF DUDLEY. Handsomely printed and bound. Fourth Impression. 7s. 6d. net.

COMMON-SENSE COOKERY. Based on Modern English and Continental Principles worked out in Detail. By Colonel A. KENNEY-HERBERT. Over 500 pages. Illustrated. 6s. net.

BY THE SAME AUTHOR.

FIFTY BREAKFASTS. 2s. 6d.
FIFTY LUNCHEONS. 2s. 6d.
FIFTY DINNERS. 2s. 6d.

THE BOOK OF WINTER SPORTS. With an Introduction by the Rt. Hon. the EARL OF LYTTON, and contributions from experts in various branches of sport. Edited by EDGAR SYERS. Fully Illustrated. Demy 8vo. 15s. net.

THE COTTAGE HOMES OF ENGLAND. Charmingly Illustrated in Colour by Mrs. ALLINGHAM. With 64 Coloured Plates. 8vo. (9½ in. by 7 in.), 21s. net. Also a limited *Edition de Luxe*, 42s. net.

RUTHLESS RHYMES FOR HEARTLESS HOMES. By Colonel D. STREAMER (Captain Harry Graham). With Illustrations by G. GATHORNE HARDY. Paper boards, 2s. 6d. net.

"Billy, in one of his nice new sashes,
Fell in the fire and got burnt to ashes;
Now, although the room is growing chilly,
I haven't the heart to poke poor Billy."

LONDON: EDWARD ARNOLD, 41 & 43 MADDOX STREET, W.

www.ingramcontent.com/pod-product-compliance
Lightning Source LLC
Chambersburg PA
CBHW021110020726
47500CB00003B/687